# THE QUIET GIRL

Nichole Heydenburg

*The Quiet Girl*

# Other Books by Nichole Heydenburg

***The Long Shadow on the Stage-*** Book 1 in *The Long Shadow Thriller Series*

***The Long Shadow of Memory-*** Book 2 in *The Long Shadow Thriller Series*

***The Long Shadow of Death-*** Book 3 in *The Long Shadow Thriller Series*

Dedicated to every teenager being bullied

# THE QUIET GIRL

# Prologue

Violet reached the final door, which she assumed led to Mallory's bedroom. Violet tentatively opened the door and stepped inside. At first glance, the room appeared empty. The light was off, so Violet flicked it on, illuminating a queen-sized bed with a wrinkled blue quilt.

Someone had been sitting on it recently.

"Hello? Is anyone in here?" She stepped further into the room.

"Help..." a weak voice answered.

Violet raced into the ensuite bathroom. "Kayla? Is that you?"

"Oh my God. Kayla!" Violet rushed over to her friend and knelt on the cool tile floor in front of the tub.

Kayla was slumped over in the bathtub, holding both hands over her abdomen. Her emerald green dress was torn and blood dripped down the bottom of the bathtub, staining the pristine white surface red.

The Quiet Girl

# Chapter 1: Before Jess

*September 16, 2019*

Violet Hale's long, light brown hair fell around her like a curtain, protecting her from the probing stares of her classmates. A book lay open on the table in front of her and she read as she ate lunch by herself, just like every day since her parents had forced her to move to North Carolina. If she was honest, she was miserable. She wanted what most fifteen-year-old girls wanted—to have friends, to fit in, and to be accepted. Moving away from Michigan hadn't been easy on her. She might as well have moved to another country. She missed her old life and her best friend, Abby. Moving right before her sophomore year of high school started was her mom's fault. She worked as a marketing manager and was offered a promotion and a substantial raise if she agreed to move. Her dad was a dentist, and he had no trouble finding a job in their new town.

Violent glanced at her phone; she had only a few minutes left for lunch. She stood, placed her book in her backpack, then slung her bag over her shoulder. Almost immediately after standing, Mallory came toward her, like a lioness stalking her prey. They were in the same grade and Mallory loved to torment her. She flicked her jet-black hair over her shoulder and stared at Violet with icy blue eyes.

Violet gulped and hurried to the trash can, tossing her garbage and silently praying that Mallory would ignore her this time. She avoided making eye contact with her again and tightened her grip on her backpack. How could someone who was easily several inches shorter than her make her feel so small? It was unfortunate that she and Mallory shared the same lunch period. It made it that much harder to avoid her tormentor.

Violet tried to head toward the cafeteria doors, but Mallory blocked her exit. Violet's pulse quickened, and she froze; she couldn't make herself move, couldn't shove Mallory out of the way or try to walk around her. It was hopeless. She only prayed it wouldn't be as bad this time. She wondered how many people were already watching the scenario play out.

"*Violet*," Mallory said in a condescending tone.

Violet finally looked up and tried her best to hide her shaking hands. "Yeah?" she said with more courage than she felt.

Mallory crossed her arms over her designer sweater and seemed to change tactics. "What were you reading?"

Violet paused. *What? Was this a trap?*

"Well? Are you going to answer me or keep standing there like a stupid bitch?"

Violet's cheeks heated as a few people giggled at the table nearby. "*A Good Girl's Guide to Murder*," she mumbled.

"What did you say? You talk so quietly no one can hear you. No wonder no one pays attention to you," Mallory retorted with a smirk.

"*A Good Girl's Guide to Murder*," Violet said more audibly.

Mallory's smirk vanished, and she wrinkled her tiny nose. "What the hell? Ew, that's so creepy. Why would you want to read something like that?"

Violet couldn't help herself and snickered at Mallory's reaction. It was nice watching her squirm for a change.

Mallory frowned and uncrossed her arms from her chest. "Did you just laugh at me? Do you really think that was a smart idea?"

At that moment, Mallory's posse joined in and stood protectively at her side, all five of them glaring at Violet. Violet had learned that Mallory was the one in charge. Then there was Jack, Mallory's twin brother, a talented musician with a long black ponytail. Next, there was Savannah, who had red hair down to her butt and had been Mallory's best friend since preschool. Rose had light brown skin and thick, dark brown hair to her shoulders. The last member was Isabelle, who went by Izzy and towered over the other girls in their school.

*Where are the teachers when I need them?* Violet glanced around to see if any of them were in the cafeteria. There should be at least two there during each lunch period to monitor the students.

The Fierce Five, as Violet referred to them, all moved in her direction, closing in on her. *Oh my God, what are they going to do to me? Why won't someone help me?*

Violet trembled and contemplated running, but they were blocking the only exit. If she turned around, she would be stuck in the cafeteria, and the lunch period was almost over. She panicked as she thought about being late for class. She was never late for anything.

Izzy spoke. "Why do you read that creepy shit? You're such a freak." She stepped forward and shoved Violet.

Violet stumbled, but caught herself before she fell. She turned around, deciding she didn't want to deal with them and would rather be late for class than have something worse happen. Violet noticed Savannah try to grab Izzy to stop her, but Izzy escaped her clutches. Izzy pushed Violet from behind, causing her to trip and fall forward, landing on her hands and knees on the sticky cafeteria floor. Her backpack fell from her shoulder and she scrambled to grab it before Mallory could try to take it. Snickers echoed from all around the room.

Violet's face burned as she stood, and her legs trembled. She could barely find the strength to get to her feet. A sophomore boy she had noticed around school walked over to them. His brown hair curled adorably around his ears and his green eyes seemed to see into her soul. He held out his hand, and she stared, not knowing what to do.

"I'm Jess," he said with a hesitant smile.

"Violet," she replied, shaking his hand limply.

"Don't let them get to you. They're all bitches," he said loudly, as a grin spread across his face.

Izzy rolled her eyes and Mallory scoffed as she glared at them.

"Oh, how the mighty have fallen," Mallory called out to Jess. Then she turned to address Violet. "Don't fool yourself. You could never get a guy like Jess."

The bell rang, and lunch was over. The group dispersed through the doorway.

"I'll walk you to class?" Jess offered.

All Violet could do was nod in response and smile shyly. She didn't even care about Mallory's rude remark. All she could think about was how cute Jess's curly brown hair was and how she hoped she didn't screw this up. Whatever it was.

*Oh my God! Why is he talking to me? What am I supposed to say?*

"You're new here, right?" Jess asked as they walked side-by-side to her English classroom.

Violet nodded and avoided eye contact.

"How do you like Asheville so far?"

At this, she sighed, unable to hide her resentment for the city where she didn't belong.

Jess laughed. "That bad, huh?"

"I miss my friends," she replied softly.

"Yeah, I can understand how that would be hard. Where did you move from?"

"Michigan."

"Oh. Too far to visit much."

"Yeah," Violet responded, finally looking at Jess in a daze as they stopped in front of her English classroom. She was already late, but she didn't want to leave him.

"This is my next class."

"Okay. Wanna eat lunch with me tomorrow?"

She stared at him, wondering if she was dreaming or imagining it all. She did that sometimes—pictured her life the way she wished it was, so she didn't have to deal with reality. Her parents always said her head was in the clouds, but most of the time, it was the only way she could survive—to pretend her life was the way it appeared in her dreams.

"Sure," she replied with a small smile.

"Cool, see you then." He waved as he walked down the hallway, presumably to his next class.

When he was gone, Violet allowed herself to smile fully before opening the classroom door. Maybe Asheville wasn't so bad after all.

\*\*\*

The next twenty-four hours passed in a blur as she eagerly awaited meeting Jess for lunch the following day. She barely paid attention in her classes and ignored her parents when they asked about school. Her older brother, Glenn, called her a zombie when he passed her the meatloaf at dinner. She accidentally dropped the heavy platter because she wasn't paying attention.

Thankfully, her younger sister, Emilia, who preferred to be called Em, chattered throughout dinner about the upcoming cheerleading tryouts at her middle school. Her inane chatter was a welcome distraction. From the sound of it, even though school had barely started, Em was already popular and would most likely make the cheerleading squad. Violet wished she could make friends as easily as her outgoing little sister.

Everything in life was easy for Em. At least, that's how it appeared to Violet. Maybe that's how life was for beautiful people. While Violet worked her butt off for good grades, Em always had nearly perfect grades without seeming to study much. She had been a cheerleader at her old school. She already had boys asking her out on dates—but their parents had strict rules about not dating until high school. Em pouted every time she had to turn down a boy's invitation to hang out alone.

Glenn, on the other hand, wasn't like either of his sisters. He had graduated from high school last spring before they moved, but he didn't know what to do next. His mediocre grades and lack of extracurriculars meant he hadn't been accepted to any of the colleges he applied to, so he still lived at home. He had wanted to stay in Michigan, but without a job or any money saved, he had no option but to move to North Carolina with the rest of his family. He seemed almost as unhappy about the move as Violet. However, he had more options than Violet. He was seventeen, practically an adult, and he could get a job or apply to a local community college—there was an entire world waiting for him—but he chose to stay at home sulking about his miserable life.

After dinner, Violet went upstairs to her bedroom to do her homework. She opened her geometry textbook and scrutinized the assigned equations for the night. It was all gibberish. Math was her weakest subject. Besides, how could she possibly concentrate on geometry when the cutest boy at her new school had invited her to eat lunch with him tomorrow?

She grabbed her phone from her bedside table and sent a quick text to her friend Abby.

**Violet:** You'll never guess what happened to me today.
**Abby:** What?
**Violet:** I met a cute guy at school. His name is Jess. :)
**Abby:** OMG! Tell me everything!
**Violet:** He walked me to class and invited me to eat lunch

with him tomorrow.

**Abby:** Vi, that's awesome! Sounds like things are looking up for you. Let me know how it goes tomorrow.

Violet returned her attention to her homework. After a few hours of boring geometry, she turned on the TV in her bedroom. She scrolled through Netflix and clicked on *Gilmore Girls*, one of her favorite comfort shows. While watching the episode when Dean and Rory kissed for the first time, Violet wondered what it would feel like to kiss Jess.

***

*September 17, 2019*

The next day, the first few hours of school seemed to drag by as if time had slowed down to half-speed. Violet kept anxiously checking the time and waiting for the lunch bell to ring. When it finally did, she bolted out of class. She had packed her things several minutes before the end of class, despite her teacher's warning that class wasn't over.

Violet was the first one out of the classroom. As she practically ran down the hallway, she realized people were staring at her like she was crazy. Her cheeks heated, and she slowed down, trying to force herself to walk at a normal pace. When she entered the cafeteria, she waited in the line for a slice of pizza. She had already analyzed her lunch options for the best choice. This was her first time eating lunch with a boy, and she didn't want to embarrass herself. She hadn't considered the pizza grease, though, so she hastily grabbed a fork and knife. Would that make her look weird? What if Jess thought she was a pig for eating pizza and not like a salad or a grilled chicken wrap?

She froze in the line before someone behind her prodded her roughly in the back.

"Can you hurry up?" they rudely said.

"Uh, sorry," Violet mumbled. She paid for the pizza and a soda and headed over to the drink station to fill her empty cup.

After the lid was securely on the cup, she scanned the room for Jess. Did he sit at the same table every day? What were his friends like? She hoped they liked her.

She spotted him at the same table as yesterday, by the windows that overlooked the grassy courtyard outside. As she approached the table, she swore everyone in the room could hear her heart thudding erratically. She thought her heart would explode at the thought of eating lunch with someone she found attractive. She idly wondered if all girls her age were this nervous around boys or if it was yet another symptom of her anxiety.

"Hey," Jess greeted her with a warm smile as she set her tray down. He was at the table by himself.

"Hi." Violet sat across from him.

After Violet had settled into a spot, a girl of average height with purple hair plopped down next to Jess, looked at Violet, then raised an eyebrow.

"Hi?"

Jess chuckled. "Sorry, Kayla. This is Violet. She's new here, and Mallory has been bothering her, so I invited her to eat lunch with us."

Kayla nodded slowly and peered at Jess before making direct eye contact with Violet. "Nice to meet you." She picked up her burger and took a huge bite. Ketchup dripped down her chin and she swiped it away with a napkin, as if it wasn't a big deal.

"Nice to meet you too," Violet replied with a tentative smile.

Violet wondered who Kayla was to Jess. A friend? A girlfriend? Friends with benefits? How could she find out?

Violet hesitantly picked up her pizza slice and took a few dainty bites. She felt self-conscious when she realized Kayla was staring at her.

Kayla's burger was already almost gone. "Sorry to hear about that bitch targeting you. What did you do to piss her off?"

"She's had it out for me since we met on the first day of school," Violet said, setting her pizza down. "All I did was accidentally bump into her."

"Seriously?" Kayla shook her head. "She's the worst. Jess would know," she added with a glance at Jess.

Jess frowned at Kayla. "Don't," he warned.

Kayla shrugged. "So, if you want to be friends with us, let me get a few things out in the open."

Jess groaned dramatically. "Come on, give her a break. You don't need to start in with all that stuff now."

"What stuff?" Violet asked, looking back and forth between Jess and Kayla.

"Kayla, cut it out. You're going to scare her away."

Kayla smiled sweetly and leaned in across the table. "If you could have one thing, what would it be? What's your deep, dark desire? Even if it's something bad. And be honest."

"You just met her. She's not going to be able to answer that yet. At least, not honestly." Jess glanced at Violet. "You can ignore her."

But something about Kayla made her want to answer honestly. Kayla seemed confident, and cool, and Jess clearly liked her—whether romantically or otherwise, that remained to be seen—either way, she wanted to fit in. She wanted to be friends with them. It was the only promising option. She didn't want to spend the next three years stuck in a town, hating her life.

"I want Mallory dead," Violet blurted out without thinking. She immediately regretted her brutal honesty. What had she been thinking? "I mean—"

Kayla laughed and rolled her eyes as she finished her burger. "You and half the school, probably." She paused, sizing up Violet, and Jess nodded. "We can make that happen."

Violet gripped her lunch tray until her knuckles turned white and glanced at both Jess and Kayla, trying to determine what they were thinking. Was this some kind of joke? Why had she said that? It was a stupid answer, so now they were treating her like she was stupid.

"I was kidding," Violet said with a weak laugh. She tried to loosen her fingers from the tray.

Jess smirked. "Well, we aren't."

"What—what do you mean?" Violet asked. "You can't just—"

"Can't what? Kill someone?" Jess asked.

"We all have someone we wish was dead. Someone who deserves it. If you help us with our darkest desires, then we'll help you with yours," Kayla said, her eyes wide.

"You can't be serious," Violet said, no longer worrying about her food choices, making friends, or whether Jess liked her. It all seemed pointless now compared to this monumental thing they were discussing in the middle of a high school cafeteria.

"Should we be talking about this here?" Jess asked, surreptitiously searching the area to see if anyone appeared to be eavesdropping. "It's not safe to talk about with so many witnesses."

Kayla crossed her arms over her chest. "Fine. We can talk about it more after school. Meet us in the parking lot. Can I see your phone?"

"Why?" Violet asked as a dozen other questions flew through her head.

"To give you my phone number, duh."

Kayla held out her hand expectantly, and Violet passed her the phone.

"There. Text me when you're ready to leave, and we'll meet in the parking lot." Kayla handed the phone back.

"You can drive?" Violet couldn't stop herself from asking.

Jess snickered. "She was held back freshman year, so she's already sixteen."

Kayla punched him roughly on the arm. "You asshole."

The bell rang to signal the end of lunch. Jess and Kayla gathered the rest of their lunches and stood to leave, staring down at Violet, who was still sitting numbly at the table.

*What the hell just happened?*

# Chapter 2: After Jess

*September 17, 2019*

While Violet sat in the back row of Mr. Pombom's English class, her mind raced as she thought about her conversation with Jess and Kayla. As a chronic overthinker, she had imagined at least twenty different scenarios for her lunch with Jess. Even in her craziest musings, she had never considered what actually happened. She contemplated texting Abby, but wasn't sure what to say. The cute guy and his friend she barely knew wanted to help her kill her bully? She shook her head, knowing she couldn't tell anyone. She would have to wait and see what happened after school.

But she couldn't stop the fear from entering her mind. What if it was a trap, and they were going to hurt her? Or worse yet, maybe it was all a setup, an elaborate ploy that Mallory and her friends were involved in? She wouldn't put it past them to go to such lengths. She thought they would do anything they could to humiliate her and destroy the little self-worth she had left.

Violet suddenly noticed Mr. Pombom's tiny dark eyes focused on her. He appeared to be waiting for her to say something.

*Shit. Did he ask me a question while I wasn't paying attention?*

She scrambled to open her paperback copy of the novella *Strange Case of Dr Jekyll and Mr Hyde* by Robert Louis Stevenson. The first two chapters had been the assigned reading for last night's homework. Violet had already read the entire novella.

"Um," she hesitated, not wanting to look dumb. But it was too late for that.

Mr. Pombom sighed in frustration. "Please, pay attention, Ms. Hale. These questions will be on the quiz on Friday."

Violet's face reddened in mortification. "Sorry," she mumbled. "Can you repeat the question, please, Mr. Pombom?"

Her English teacher peered at her with the utmost patience. "Of course. I asked you what year the book was published."

"1886," Violet replied instantly, pleased that she knew the answer. Her English literature class was her favorite.

Mr. Pombom nodded in acknowledgement and moved on with his lecture.

Violet sighed, relieved, and tried her best to pay attention. She didn't want her grades to suffer, especially since the school year had only started a few weeks ago. She couldn't make a poor impression so early in the semester.

Twenty minutes later, Violet's English class ended, and she headed to Spanish. She wanted to take French, but her parents insisted Spanish would be more useful. She dreamed of visiting Paris someday and wished she was learning French instead. To make matters worse, Mallory was in her Spanish class. Yet another reason French would have been better. Violet hoped Señora Iliza never paired them up for a project; that would be her luck.

She sat through another endless lecture given by Señora Iliza. She was an older teacher close to retirement, and she didn't seem to know how to keep the students' attention. Maybe she didn't care. Unfortunately, they didn't practice speaking the language, so most of what she droned on about didn't sink in.

When Spanish ended, Violet went to her locker to grab her other textbooks, thankful the school day was over. She sent a quick text to her dad to tell him she was hanging out with friends after school. He instantly replied, telling her to be safe and have fun.

Her mom was still at work and never checked her phone during the day, so telling her dad was good enough. Her mom probably didn't care. When Violet was in third grade, she broke her arm during recess, trying to hang upside down on the monkey bars. Her dad was in the middle of an intensive dental surgery. However, her mom hadn't answered the dozen phone calls from the school, so her dad had stopped the surgery to pick Violet up from school.

That was only one of many times her dad had ceased everything to be there for his kids, while their mom had been off in her own world. She was preoccupied with how being a married woman with kids affected her job and how her coworkers saw her.

Next, she texted Kayla.

**Violet:** Hi, it's Violet. I'm out of class and heading to the parking lot now.

**Kayla:** Cool. I drive a white Toyota Corolla. I'll be standing by it so you can find us.

**Violet:** Thanks, see you soon.

Violet walked toward the underclassmen parking lot, wondering how many white Corollas were parked there. Luckily, she didn't have to search for long before Kayla and Jess noticed her and waved for her to join them.

"Hey," Jess greeted her.

"Viiiolet!" Kayla said in a singsong voice.

"Uh, hi," Violet replied.

Kayla grinned mischievously. "You ready for this or what?"

"Honestly, I'm not sure." Violet's grip tightened on her backpack.

"Don't worry, tonight we aren't doing anything too dangerous," Kayla said.

Jess rolled his eyes. "We're going to a place in downtown Asheville to hang out. My parents own a coffee shop called Big Beanz Coffee."

Violet couldn't help but giggle at the name.

"Yeah, I know it's really stupid," Jess responded as he pursed his lips. "The name is so obnoxious that people always want to check it out, though, so I guess it was smart marketing or whatever."

Violet perked up at his mention of marketing. "I think you mean smart branding. That's the sort of thing my mom does. She's a marketing manager."

"Oh yeah?" Jess asked.

Kayla huffed impatiently. Violet was surprised to see Kayla already sitting in the driver's seat.

"Sorry," Jess said sheepishly.

He opened the back door for Violet and she got in with a smile. "Thanks."

Jess closed her door before walking to the passenger seat and getting in.

Kayla turned her keys in the ignition and smirked. "Did you really just open the door for her?"

"Yeah, I was being polite." Jess's face flushed. He turned away from Kayla and busied himself with buckling his seatbelt.

Kayla snorted.

Violet pulled out her cellphone, wondering if she should keep 911 dialed in case they were going to take her somewhere weird or try to hurt her. Getting into a car with two people who were essentially strangers hadn't been smart. But she was miserable and desperate for friends. Despite Kayla's tough exterior, she seemed normal. And Jess had been the one to stand up to Mallory and her friends. They couldn't be that bad, right?

Kayla backed the car out of the parking space and exited the school's parking lot. Kayla had only driven for thirty seconds before she slammed on her brakes to prevent the car from hitting one of the school buses that had stopped in front of them.

Kayla groaned. "Ugh, this is why I wanted to get out of there sooner! I knew this would happen." She banged the steering wheel with her fist. "Now we have to wait."

Jess placed a hand on Kayla's shoulder and squeezed. "I promise you'll survive."

Violet watched Jess and Kayla's interaction and wondered again if they were only friends or romantically involved. She wished she could ask in a way that wasn't completely obvious. If she brought it up, it would be apparent why she wanted to know. Then again, should she lust after Jess if he was involved in something dangerous? There were plenty of other attractive guys at her new high school, but none of them paid attention to her. In fact, some of them, like Mallory's twin brother Jack, joined in on the bullying.

"You look like you're deep in thought," Jess said as he noticed Violet's expression.

"Oh, yeah. Just a lot going on," Violet replied glumly, staring out the window.

Kayla raised an eyebrow at her. "I hope you have good taste in music because I've got a killer playlist." She handed her phone to Jess.

Jess scrolled through Kayla's phone, finding the playlist he wanted and selecting the play button after he made sure the phone had connected to the car's Bluetooth.

A familiar rock song played. Something her dad listened to. Violet nodded in recognition. "I'm good with this."

Kayla smiled and nodded back. It was probably the closest thing to acceptance she would get.

Violet pulled up Big Beanz Coffee's menu on her phone, not wanting to be forced to browse the menu hurriedly when they arrived. She scoped out a few options that sounded good and also scrolled through the coffee shop's Instagram page. She didn't like the taste of black coffee, but she could always add cream and sugar, if that's what Kayla and Jess ordered.

The school was only a few miles from the downtown area, so they didn't listen to much of the playlist before Kayla parked across the street from a coffee shop. There was a huge, colorful sign out front that said *Big Beanz Coffee.*

They entered the coffee shop, and Kayla bolted for a table near the back, yelling, "Get me my usual!"

Jess, who was already walking behind the counter, turned to look at Violet. "What do you want?"

This wasn't what she had planned. She wanted to see what they ordered first. "What are you getting?"

Kayla laughed from the table across the coffee shop, and Violet regretted the question.

Jess smiled warmly. "My go-to drink is iced coffee with caramel syrup."

Violet smiled back at him. "That sounds perfect."

"A girl after my heart," Jess teased, pressing his palm against his chest.

Violet blushed, but maintained eye contact. If she wanted him to like her, she needed to get to know him better. How could he like her if he knew nothing about her? "Do you always hang out here after school?"

"Most days, yeah," Jess said with a nod. "I'll grab some snacks too."

He disappeared into the back room, and Violet stood there awkwardly, wondering what she should do. She supposed it made sense to join Kayla at the table, but what if Jess couldn't carry everything by himself?

Kayla saved her from having to decide. She shouted from across the coffee shop, "Are you going to come sit with me, or do I have to keep sitting here alone?"

Violet sat across from Kayla at the circular wooden table, and set her backpack on the floor, wondering what to talk about. She hoped Jess would sit next to her and break the silence soon.

"How long have you known Jess?" Violet asked carefully, deciding it was a reasonably safe, normal thing to ask.

Kayla scrunched up her nose. "I've known Jess since middle school. He had a crush on me," she said and shrugged her shoulders.

"Wow, you've known each other a long time, then?"

"Yeah." Kayla tilted her head to the side as if sizing Violet up.

Violet knew it was stupid, but she couldn't stop herself. She wanted to know their history. "Did you ever have a crush on him?"

Kayla smirked. "Nope, I never thought of him that way. He's my best friend, nothing more. And he's single, if that's what you're worried about."

Violet's cheeks flamed and she tried to smooth over the awkwardness. "I was just making conversation. I didn't mean—"

"It's fine, Violet. No worries," Kayla answered with a small smile. "Besides, I think he likes you. It's nice seeing him happy again."

Violet smiled back timidly.

"So, about the reason we're here—"

Before Kayla could explain whatever was going on, Jess joined them, precariously balancing three drinks and a pile of snacks.

"Thanks for all the help!" he said with a wide, sarcastic grin. He set the drinks and snacks on the table and took the seat in between Violet and Kayla.

"Sorry!" Violet said quickly, regretting her choice to join Kayla at the table. "Thanks for the iced coffee and food."

"No problem, you can thank my parents later," he said as he slurped his iced coffee. "They'll probably come check on us soon. They would rather have us hang out here than most places, but they still don't completely trust me."

Violet's face paled. Meeting Jess's parents sounded both wonderful and terrifying. "Oh, okay." She picked up her iced coffee and took a hesitant sip. Her eyes widened, and Kayla laughed.

"What? Did you think it was going to be bad?" Kayla asked.

"No, I don't like coffee usually. It's good, though," Violet said.

Jess slurped more of his coffee. "If there's one thing my parents can do right, it's brewing great coffee. They get the beans from a local roaster."

Kayla nodded vigorously. "For sure."

Violet happily sipped her coffee and realized she was hungry. She grabbed one of the granola bars Jess had brought.

After Violet polished off the granola bar, she looked around the coffee shop more thoroughly, allowing herself to relax. It was a modern but cozy space. The tables were all the same as the circular wooden one they surrounded. Silver, globe-shaped light fixtures hung intermittently throughout the space. Artwork from local artists lined the walls, with their name, hometown, and the price listed below each one.

"It's a nice place," she told Jess.

"Thanks. My parents would love to hear that. They've put a lot of work into updating it and trying to draw in new customers."

"Well, they did a great job. I watch HGTV sometimes with my mom, so I know more than I should about popular decorating choices."

"Ah, I love the one with the attractive twin guys," Kayla said with a wink, much to Violet's surprise.

She hadn't taken her for a *Property Brothers* fan. *Looks can be deceiving*, she reminded herself. Maybe Kayla and Jess would be her new friends and her life would vastly improve here. Having people to hang out with, to eat lunch with, to talk to—it would make a world of difference. She decided to make the most of this, whatever it was.

But the one thing Violet kept wondering was whether Kayla and Jess were serious about getting revenge. Were they really planning on killing the people they didn't like? And if so, what was she going to do about it?

# Chapter 3:
# Before Jess

*August 5, 2019*

August in Asheville meant sweltering heat, and the back-to-school countdown was on. Only two weeks remained until Violet's first day at her new school, where she would be a sophomore. She was nervous about starting over in the middle of high school. She didn't make friends easily and worried about how the teenagers at her new school would act. From what she could tell from the past few weeks, Asheville was nothing like the small town she had grown up in near Grand Rapids, Michigan. Asheville locals were extremely against outsiders moving to their town. Violet stood out with her Michigan accent, and she had quickly learned that people in the south didn't say "pop" when she received a strange look in a restaurant after trying to order a Coke.

Violet slowly unpacked the boxes in her new bedroom, looking around the space that would be hers for the next three years until she went away to college. She planned on moving back to Michigan for college, going to Michigan State, and being roommates with her best friend, Abby.

She arranged some of her books on the bookshelf and stood back to admire her handiwork. A stack of boxes left to unpack taunted her, but that could wait for another day. Her phone buzzed with a text message.

> **Abby:** Hey, how's the new place?
>
> **Violet:** It's… fine. I miss you. :(
>
> **Abby:** I miss you too!! When are you going to come visit?
>
> **Violet:** I'm not sure. My parents won't give me an answer. Maybe you could come here in a few months. For Christmas or something?
>
> **Abby:** Hmm… I'm not sure my parents would let me miss a holiday with them, but I can try!
>
> **Violet:** Ugh, you better.

Violet frustratedly set her phone down and looked out the window. Night was approaching. Another night to spend in her bedroom watching Netflix or reading a new book. She hadn't been to many places since moving and didn't know anyone yet, but Violet's dad promised she wouldn't have trouble making friends when school started.

\*\*\*

*August 19, 2019*

Two weeks later, Violet entered the high school by herself and immediately felt uncomfortable. The absence of Abby's bubbly, bright self was noticeable.

Violet entered the administration office, where she had been instructed to go since she was a new student.

"Hello," the receptionist cheerfully greeted her. "How can I help you, sweetie?"

Violet frowned. She hated being called sweetie in such a condescending tone by adults. It was unnecessary and made her feel like a small child.

"Hi, my name is Violet Hale. I'm a new student."

"Oh yes, Miss Hale," the receptionist said, peering at her through her golden-rimmed glasses. "I have your paperwork somewhere around here." She glanced around the messy office.

Violet stood in front of the desk impatiently as she panicked about being late for her first class. She didn't want to make a bad first impression, but being late would probably give her a panic attack. She took a deep breath and willed herself to stay calm. *It's fine. Everything will be fine*, she tried to convince herself.

A few minutes later, the elderly receptionist turned back to face her, holding a manila folder stuffed full of documents. "Ah, here we go. Your class information, room numbers, assigned lunch period, locker number… all the important things you need to know are in here. Sorry about that. Sometimes I swear I would lose my head if it wasn't attached to me!" She gave Violet a cheesy grin, obviously expecting her to double over with laughter.

Violet laughed politely at the dumb joke and took the envelope. "Thanks."

"If you have questions, dear, you can always stop by."

Violet nodded and left the office, glancing at her phone to check the time. *Shit, only five minutes until my first class!*

She hoped her history classroom wasn't far away. She opened the envelope to look at the room number as she walked down the hallway, not paying attention to where she was headed. Suddenly, she jerked to a stop as she walked into someone's back. She hastily scrambled to apologize.

"Oh my gosh, I'm sorry!"

The girl she had bumped into turned around and glared at her with the full force of her cold blue eyes. She had glossy, shoulder-length jet black hair and was a few inches shorter than Violet, but somehow seemed intimidating as hell.

"Excuse you," the girl said, intensifying her glare.

"Sorry, I was trying to figure out where my first class is," Violet explained. "I'm new here. I didn't mean to bump into you."

A boy who looked eerily similar to the girl joined them. He had the same blue eyes and black hair, although his hair was gathered into a low ponytail hanging down his back, even longer than the girl's. Her brother, maybe?

The boy put his arm loosely around his companion's shoulders. "Coming, Mallory? Don't wanna be late on the first day. What's going on?"

"This bitch ran into me and almost knocked me over," Mallory practically spat.

Violet stared at the two teenagers, aghast at the lie. She had barely bumped into Mallory, and she definitely hadn't been close to falling over.

"You better watch it," the boy warned her. "Mallory doesn't mess around. You pissed off the wrong person." He chuckled and grabbed Mallory's arm, turning her around and walking to class.

Violet gulped. She didn't care that she still had no clue where her history class was. It was only the first day of school and two people already hated her. *Off to a great start.*

***

After the incident in the morning, most of the day passed in a blur. Violet barely made it to her first class as the bell rang, and she chose a safe seat toward the back of the classroom. Her classes seemed fine. This semester she was taking history, geometry, a fitness class, English, and Spanish.

After her fitness class, she walked to the cafeteria to eat lunch. She hadn't been brave enough to ask anyone if she could join them. She waited in line for chicken nuggets, wondering where she should sit. If this school was anything like her old one, there would be cliques. It would be impossible to get close to anyone unless she tried, but being outgoing and making friends wasn't exactly her strong suit.

After she paid for her food and a drink, she turned to face the rows of tables lining the room. Many of them were already full, but some had empty chairs. She looked back and forth between several spots, trying to decide which one was better. Finally, she lost her courage and headed toward the window at the back of the cafeteria and sat at an empty table.

When she was comfortable, she pulled her book out of her backpack and propped it open on the table in front of her. She grabbed a chicken nugget and dunked it in ketchup, then turned the page. If there was one thing Violet could always count on, it was books. Reading had been her escape since she was six. She had never made friends easily, and Abby had been her closest friend since first grade. Violet and Abby had been the only two who didn't want to play softball at recess and opted to stay inside and read. The two young girls spent most of that day talking about their favorite books, their siblings, how much they hated sports, and how much they loved pizza and the color purple.

They became fast friends after that. It seemed so easy back then, when something as small as having the same favorite color could result in a friendship. In high school, it was all about fitting in and being cool. So, how was she supposed to make friends if she didn't fit in?

Violet flipped the page of her book and shoved another ketchup-slathered chicken nugget into her mouth. It was only the first day of school. Whatever happened, at least she had chicken nuggets. Surely, the incident with that girl Mallory would blow over and everything would be fine. It had been an accident. And accidents were meant to be forgiven.

# Chapter 4: After Jess

*September 17, 2019*

In the coffee shop, Violet expected Kayla or Jess to bring up their secret plan or whatever they had alluded to earlier. Instead, Kayla talked about taking down the patriarchy and how feminists needed to rise up and take control of the government. She seemed to think a female president would fix the country. Then Kayla and Jess both went off on a tangent, talking about how Morrissey *really* was too old to be touring, but they would still attend a show if he had a concert in Asheville. Violet simply listened to their conversation, wondering what she could contribute. She was all for feminism, and she didn't mind Morrissey's music, but she didn't know what to say.

Kayla stopped talking and slurped her coffee, which she must have realized was empty. She shook the plastic cup around and the sound of the ice cubes clanging together grated Violet's nerves. She couldn't stand unnecessary noise.

"What do you think, Violet?" Kayla asked.

Violet was caught off guard. "About what?"

"Well, anything really. You're so—"

"Quiet? Yeah, I get that a lot," Violet responded snarkily. She folded her arms defensively across her chest—her signature move when she was uncomfortable.

"Sorry, I didn't mean anything by it. It's fine." Kayla set down her empty coffee cup and grabbed a bag of chips.

"Yeah, it's refreshing," Jess chimed in, looking at her with a smile that crinkled his green eyes irresistibly.

"Okay." What else was she supposed to say to that? She was quiet, but she was sick of everyone always pointing it out like it mattered whether she was an introvert or an extrovert. Couldn't she just be a person and feel comfortable being herself for once? Couldn't people accept her the way she was and not always try to force her to be someone else?

Jess placed his hand gently on her arm. "Hey, we aren't judging you, I promise. We've both been judged enough at school. We know what it's like, so we would never do that to someone."

"Unless they deserved it, of course," Kayla retorted, twirling her purple hair around her finger.

"Right," Jess agreed.

Just then, a petite woman with blonde hair walked out of the backroom and toward their table. She was carrying a large platter that contained an assortment of cookies.

"Well, hello, everyone," she said with a kind smile.

She set the platter on the table, and Jess immediately ogled the cookies.

"Hi, Mrs. Woodfield," Kayla answered in a polite voice that Violet had never heard her use.

Mrs. Woodfield turned to Violet with an outstretched hand. "You must be Violet. Nice to meet you. I'm Jess's mom. You can call me Jasmine."

Violet shook her hand. "Nice to meet you, too."

"So, you and your family recently moved here?" Jasmine asked. "How do you like Asheville?"

"Yes, we moved here at the beginning of August. It's... really different from Michigan," Violet answered honestly.

"I bet. Jess's father, Christopher, and I have been to the Upper Peninsula a few times for vacations. Lovely place."

"Oh yeah, the U.P... uh, that's what we call it... the Upper Peninsula is beautiful," Violet stuttered.

Jasmine smiled. "I hope you aren't having too difficult of a time adjusting. It seems like you're having no trouble making friends," she said with a nod toward Jess and Kayla.

Violet's cheeks reddened. She didn't know if they considered her to be their friend yet. "Uh, yeah."

"Well, I wanted to welcome you to the town, and I brought these cookies over for you all to enjoy." Jasmine gave Jess a pointed look. "Save some for your friends, Jess."

Jess had already eaten at least two of the cookies.

Kayla grabbed one that looked like it had chocolate chips in it.

"What kind are they?" Violet asked hesitantly as she scanned the assortment.

Jasmine gasped and held her hand to her mouth; her eyes widened in concern. "Oh shit, I didn't ask if you had any food allergies! I'm so sorry. You don't, do you?"

"No, I don't," Violet replied with an awkward laugh.

"Oh, thank goodness," Jasmine stood with her hand on her hip, pointing at each cookie as she spoke. "Those are chocolate chip. Those are peanut butter, M&M, snickerdoodle, and oatmeal raisin…" she hesitated. "Yes, oatmeal raisin," she finished with a confident nod.

Jess grabbed his third cookie, and Jasmine shot him an angry look. "Jess! Slow down and let your friends have some cookies. I didn't make them for you." She rolled her eyes and walked away. "Nice meeting you, Violet. You're welcome by here anytime!"

"Thank you!" Violet called back, straining her quiet voice to be heard.

She chose an M&M cookie and bit into it. It was warm and gooey; the M&Ms were melting. They must have been fresh out of the oven. "Your mom seems nice," she said to Jess as she chewed the cookie.

Jess nodded as he ate what was probably his fourth or fifth cookie.

Kayla started laughing and Violet looked at her, wondering what was so funny.

Kayla covered her mouth to finish chewing her cookie before she spoke. "Jess, you have zero self-control." She shook her head. "If you want to know the way to win him over, it's with baked goods," Kayla said with an evil grin.

Violet's face reddened for the dozenth time that day, but when she glanced at Jess, he seemed oblivious to Kayla's comment. *Thank God.*

Violet wondered if she should ask Kayla for a ride home or if that was rude. She didn't want to leave yet, but she had homework due tomorrow. She didn't want to get behind on her schoolwork if she started having a social life.

"How late were you guys planning on hanging out here?" Violet asked.

Jess paused from shoving cookies into his mouth and wiped crumbs from his shirt. "At least another hour, probably. It's not too late yet." He glanced at the time on his phone. "Why?"

Violet hesitated. "My parents expect me to be home for dinner."

Jess seemed to straighten his posture, and Kayla shot him a meaningful look. Violet wondered what the look was about.

"But we haven't talked about—" Kayla protested.

"Shh!" Jess interrupted her. "We can't talk about that in here. My parents could be listening."

"Okay, okay. Chill. We can go somewhere else to talk," Kayla said nonchalantly. "Why did we come here, then?"

Jess held up a cookie. "For snacks, obviously."

Violet bit her lip anxiously. "Could we talk about whatever it is tomorrow instead? I need to get home soon. I have tons of homework to do tonight."

Jess nodded. "Of course. Kayla can take you home."

Kayla shot him a look but complied. "Sure, I'll take you home. I guess I should go home soon and do homework too. It's the responsible thing to do. Although, it might be difficult to concentrate if he is over again." She sighed dramatically.

Jess nodded as if he knew what Kayla meant.

"Who?" Violet asked curiously.

"Um, I'll tell you some other time," Kayla answered.

Violet gathered her belongings and grabbed another cookie. "Well, let your mom know the cookies were delicious. See you at school tomorrow?"

"I'll tell her. See you tomorrow." Jess waved goodbye.

Kayla grabbed her backpack. "Let's get going then. Bye Jess."

Violet followed Kayla to her car, opened the passenger door, and settled into the seat, trying not to appear nervous. Jess wasn't coming with them. She didn't know what to talk about, and she didn't know if Kayla liked her. The car ride would be interesting, to say the least.

After Kayla backed out of the parking space and they were on the road, she asked where Violet lived. Violet still didn't know her way around town, so she entered her address into Google Maps and navigated. Her house was about fifteen minutes from the coffee shop.

Violet glanced at Kayla, who was concentrating on driving and hadn't spoken since Violet started giving her directions.

Kayla smirked when she noticed Violet staring at her. "You're wondering about what we mentioned at lunch yesterday, aren't you?"

"Uh… I mean, yeah."

Kayla paused. "I know you haven't lived here long, so you probably aren't aware of all the high school gossip yet, but Jess went through a rough break-up about a year ago," She hesitated as if choosing her words carefully. "The break-up was really hard on him. His ex-girlfriend cheated on him and ended things publicly."

"Who?"

Was it someone she knew? Someone who went to their school, maybe? She tried to picture Jess with any of the girls she had met, but she didn't like the idea. Plus, who would be cruel enough to cheat on him and then break up publicly? That sounded like a terrible thing to go through.

Kayla shook her head, refusing to give a straight answer. "It doesn't matter. The point is that it took months for Jess to be himself again. It almost destroyed him. When he was at his lowest point, he mentioned something to me. An idea about bringing our deepest, darkest desires to fruition. On the surface, he wanted revenge for the break-up. But really, he wanted an excuse to act on his dark desires. I think that's what most of us want deep down. There's someone I want revenge on, too. Someone who... hurt me." She tilted her head to the side and glanced at Violet.

Violet paused, wondering if she should even ask, but she did anyway. Kayla had been the one to bring it up, after all.

"If Jess wants revenge on his ex, then what about you? Who's your target?"

"My mom's boyfriend."

That hadn't been the answer Violet expected. "Why? What did he do?"

Kayla shook her head emphatically. "I don't want to talk about it. Maybe after—"

"It's fine. You don't have to tell me. We don't know each other very well yet." Violet attempted to change the subject. "So, what did Jess do after his ex broke up with him?"

"Nothing yet. We wanted to be careful while we came up with a foolproof plan, so nothing could be traced back to us. We're being cautious so we can get away with it. So far, there are a few steps to the plan."

Violet twirled her hair around her finger. Kayla was being purposely vague. She hadn't mentioned the name of Jess's ex. She hadn't explained the details of their plan. And she also noticed that Kayla had conveniently left out what her mom's boyfriend did. Why did she want revenge on him? Did she want to kill him? Was Violet becoming friends with two potential murderers?

Violet was consumed with the mystery involving Jess and Kayla's dark desires and barely noticed that Kayla had pulled her car into her driveway and put the car in park.

"I promise we'll tell you more. We want to get to know you first and make sure you're cut out for this."

"You don't trust me yet," Violet said with an uneasy smile. She wasn't sure she trusted them either, even if she was attracted to Jess. Thinking someone was cute was completely different from trusting them. She barely knew Jess and Kayla.

"It's not just that. And don't mention anything about the break-up to Jess. He wouldn't be happy I told you. He doesn't like re-living it and gets worked up every time someone brings it up."

"Don't worry, I won't say anything." She grabbed her backpack and opened the passenger door, exiting the car. "Thanks for the ride."

Kayla waved her fingers at her. "No problem."

\*\*\*

While Violet did her homework that night, her thoughts continuously strayed to what Kayla had told her. Now she knew one of Jess's secrets. She was glad Kayla had trusted her enough to reveal a tiny piece of their world. All she had to do now was wait until she found out what they were up to. She remained unconvinced that she wanted to be involved in their secret plan. It could be dangerous, and she didn't want to get in trouble. Besides, what did Kayla mean by 'deep, dark desires?' She wasn't sure she wanted to know. But she was desperate for friends, desperate to belong, and maybe desperate enough to let herself get wrapped up in something crazy.

# Chapter 5:
# Before Jess

*August 19, 2019*

When Violet entered her Spanish class on the first day of school, she immediately wanted to turn and run. Mallory was already sitting in the back row. She was talking to a girl with thick, dark brown hair to her shoulders, light brown skin, and a heart-shaped face. Mallory was laughing, but the girl she was talking to looked uncomfortable. Unfortunately, there weren't many empty seats left, so she was forced to take the seat directly in front of them. She swore she could feel Mallory's glare pierce her back like a dagger. She felt extremely self-conscious as she pulled out a notebook and pencil from her backpack and prepared for class.

The Spanish teacher, Señora Iliza, began class with one of those panic-inducing icebreakers that teachers think are helpful. She wanted each student to say their name and three facts about themselves. Violet rapidly tapped her pencil on the desk as she considered which three facts she could tell the entire class. She didn't think she was interesting. Some students were already saying cool things, like one guy who said he went to Paris or a girl who claimed she met Tom Holland and got his signature.

When it was Violet's turn, she noticed sweat had soaked through her carefully chosen maroon babydoll top and she tried her best to keep her arms by her sides so the sweat wasn't obvious to everyone else.

"Hi, I'm Violet," she mumbled.

Señora Iliza immediately said, "Speak up, so the students in the front row can hear you too!"

She cleared her throat. "I'm Violet," she repeated. "I moved here from Michigan over the summer. I have a younger sister and an older brother. And… I was on the dance team at my old school." The words tumbled out quickly.

Violet heard giggles behind her and assumed it was Mallory and her friend making fun of her.

When it was Mallory's turn, Violet hesitantly turned around to hear her introduction.

"Most of you know me. I'm Mallory," Mallory said with a fake smile, the type of smile a politician would give when trying to win over new voters. "I have a twin brother named Jack. My favorite place I've traveled to is Barbados. Last, I plan on attending Brown for college." She finished with a self-satisfied smile that implied everyone should be impressed.

Señora Iliza nodded and gestured for Mallory's friend to go next.

The brown-haired girl waved her large hand. "I'm Rose. My favorite food is ice cream. I hope to be a chef someday. My mom is from Spain, but my dad is American. I have dual citizenship. Plus, I'm fluent in Spanish, so this class should be easy," she said with a big grin.

The last few students told the class their interesting facts, and Señora Iliza gave them a basic Spanish quiz to determine how much they already knew about the language. While Violet concentrated on the quiz and tried to remember the Spanish word for "pencil," a sharp stab pierced the middle of her back and she winced.

Several students turned to scrutinize her curiously, and Violet sank lower in her seat. Had Mallory poked her in the back? With what, though? And better yet, why?

Another stabbing sensation pierced her back, this time more painfully, and she yelped. "Ow!" she gasped and covered her mouth with her hand, then turned around to look at Mallory, who quickly averted her eyes and pretended to be working on her quiz.

Señora Iliza strode over to Violet's desk. "Ms. Hale, what on earth is the matter?" she asked with annoyance.

"Um, nothing. Just dealing with some back pain," Violet explained. It wasn't necessarily a lie.

"Do you need to go see the nurse?" Señora Iliza asked as she raised an eyebrow.

"No, I'll be fine."

"All right then, please control yourself and remain quiet, so you don't disturb your classmates who are diligently working on their quizzes," Señora Iliza said with a noticeable look and approving smile toward Mallory.

*You've got to be fucking kidding me.*

\*\*\*

Violet walked toward her mom's large black SUV with overwhelming relief that the day was over. Violet carefully sat in the car and tried not to be obvious about her back pain.

"How was your first day?" her mom asked excitedly as soon as Violet had her seatbelt on.

Violet avoided looking directly at her mom. "Fine."

"Did you make any friends? Do you like your classes?"

"Yes."

Her mom looked at her and scrunched her eyebrows together. "Are you all right, Vi?"

Violet rolled her eyes. "I'm fine, Mom."

Her mom tapped her fingers on the steering wheel as she drove. "Okay."

Before they could go home, they needed to pick up her younger sister, Emilia, from middle school. The middle school started a half hour later than the high school, so the pick-up time was also later. Since Violet wasn't sixteen yet and didn't have her driver's license, it worked out that her mom could pick them up from school and not have to worry about either of them waiting to be picked up. Today was a rare instance when their mom was the one chauffeuring them around. Her afternoon meeting was canceled. Usually, their dad was the one who drove them around. The only plus side was that they didn't have to ride the bus, although sometimes it felt more embarrassing to still be dropped off and picked up everywhere by her parents.

After Emilia jumped into the backseat of the car—one perk of Violet being picked up first was that she automatically got to ride shotgun—Emilia instantly launched into story after story about her first day of eighth grade. She would join Violet at the high school next year, which was weird. Unlike her, Emilia could become friends with anyone because she was good at talking to people and figuring out things they had in common. Violet envied her easygoing personality and often wished she had half of Emilia's self-confidence.

"How was your day, Vi?" Emilia asked, abruptly stopping in the middle of her story about how excited she was for cheerleading tryouts.

"Fine," Violet said in a monotone, echoing the response she gave her mom.

Emilia frowned. She may have been more popular, confident, and easygoing than Violet, but she certainly wasn't dumb. And she cared about her sister. "What happened?" she asked knowingly.

Their mom pursed her lips as she pulled the SUV into the garage at their new house. "Vi doesn't want to talk about it."

The second their mom parked the car, Violet jumped out with her backpack in her hands before the car was turned off. She ran into the house, up the stairs to her bedroom, and shut the door.

She had barely set down her backpack and settled under the quilt on her bed before there was a knock on the door.

"Yeah?" Violet yelled in irritation.

"It's me," Emilia said. "Can I come in?" She shoved the door open before Violet could say no.

Violet huddled under the covers on her bed, the blanket over her face, wanting to hide from the world. Emilia sat next to her on the bed.

"What's wrong?" She yanked the quilt off of Violet's face. "You can talk to me. I won't tell Mom and Dad if you don't want me to."

Violet folded her arms on top of the quilt. "It was a bad first day. I'll be fine."

Emilia hesitated, probably wondering if she was being honest. "Well, okay, everyone has bad days once in a while. Promise that's it, and nothing really awful happened?"

Violet nodded, hoping her sister would take the hint and give up.

Emilia lifted the quilt and slid under it, propping herself up with one of Violet's extra pillows. "Let's watch a movie until dinner's ready."

Violet shrugged. Emilia picked up the remote and scrolled through Netflix. While Emilia was paying attention to Netflix, Violet compared herself to her sister for the dozenth time that day. A silent tear slid down her cheek and she hastily brushed it away, not wanting Emilia to see her cry. She was intent on convincing herself that everything was okay, like she had promised her mom and Emilia, even if it felt like nothing was going right.

If only Violet had known then that things would only get worse.

# Chapter 6: After Jess

*September 18, 2019*

On most mornings, Violet was the type of person who jumped out of bed the moment her alarm went off, but lately, she dreaded leaving the comfort of her bed. It meant she had to go to school and face her tormentors. Things would have been easier if Mallory and Rose weren't in her Spanish class or if Mallory and her friends didn't all share the same lunch period as she did, but unfortunately, that wasn't the world she lived in.

With a weary sigh, she dragged herself out of her cocoon of blankets and stumbled to the bathroom she shared with Emilia. Her sister's earth-shattering snores and alarm blared through Emilia's closed door. Emilia always slept through her alarm, no matter how obnoxious it was. Violet didn't know how she did it. The tiniest noise could wake her up.

She showered, blow-dried her hair, dabbed a bit of mascara on her eyelashes, and then put on the outfit she had laid out the night before. As Violet left the bathroom, Emilia stumbled in with her frizzy, dark blonde hair a tangled mess, sleepily rubbing her eyes.

"Morning, Vi," Emilia mumbled as she grabbed her toothbrush.

"Morning, Em."

Violet headed downstairs to the kitchen where her mom was pouring coffee into her thermos. Her mom turned to face her when she opened the pantry to grab a granola bar.

Her mom frowned. "That's not a very nutritious breakfast. Do you want some eggs?" She glanced at the clock above the stove. "Never mind, it's too late. Where's your sister? We need to get going."

Violet shrugged. "She woke up late again. She was brushing her teeth when I came down, but she wasn't even dressed yet."

Her mom glared at her. "Violet! Why didn't you wake her up?!" Her mom stormed up the stairs, yelling for Emilia to hurry.

"How is that my fault?" Violet muttered after her mom was out of earshot.

Thirty minutes later, Violet exited her mom's SUV in front of the high school.

"Bye! Have a good day!" her mom called after her as Violet shut the passenger door.

Violet waved halfheartedly at her mom and sister and headed toward the school's entrance. As she walked, someone tapped her shoulder, and she whipped around, her brown eyes wild with fear.

It was Jess. He smiled and then laughed at her expression. "Sorry, did I scare you?"

"Just a little." Violet tried to calm her racing heart rate and stop the 'fight or flight' instinct that had kicked her adrenaline into overdrive.

"Was that your mom and sister in the car?" Jess asked.

"Yeah. Emilia goes to the middle school. She's in eighth grade, so she'll be here next year."

Jess's eyes widened. "Whoa. She does *not* look like a middle schooler."

Violet wasn't sure what to think about that, so she bit her lip, stalling for a response. She knew Emilia was much prettier than she was and assumed that was what Jess thought too. Although, as she thought about it more, it seemed a bit creepy if he thought about a thirteen-year-old that way.

"I mean, she looks older than that," Jess explained as his cheeks flushed. "I wasn't trying to be creepy!" he added as if he knew what she was thinking.

Violet gave him the side-eye and proceeded into the school.

"Wait, Violet! Where are you going?" Jess yelled, trying to catch up to her fast stride.

She stopped and turned around to glare at him. "To class?" she said sarcastically.

The smile dropped from Jess's face, and he touched her arm lightly. "Hey, is everything all right?"

"I'm fine," Violet retorted, shaking off his hand.

"Well, it sure doesn't seem like it. I was going to ask if you wanted to meet up with me and Kayla after school today." He smiled hesitantly.

"I don't think that's a good idea."

"Why not? It seemed like you had fun with us last night," Jess said as his smile vanished.

Violet shook her head. "Kayla and I talked on the way home yesterday. She told me—" Violet hesitated, wondering if she should break her promise to Kayla about not bringing up the break-up.

"What?" Jess said, his voice sharp. He stood in front of her now, blocking her path.

"It doesn't matter. I can't talk about it."

"What did Kayla tell you, Violet?" Jess demanded.

"Never mind. I have to get to history."

"Let me walk you there, at least."

Violet faced him and stared at him boldly. She wanted answers and didn't want to continue pining after Jess if he didn't reciprocate her feelings. "Why?"

Jess's eyebrows scrunched together. "What do you mean, *why*? I'm being nice."

"Oh." Although it wasn't unexpected, it wasn't the answer she wanted. She wanted him to say that he thought she was pretty, and he wanted to be with her. But was that realistic? Probably not. She sighed in resignation. "Fine, walk me to class then."

She grabbed his arm and pulled him inside. He stumbled along behind her as they entered the school. Once they had moved past the entrance and down the hallway, she let go of his arm.

"You sure everything's good?" Jess appraised her and rubbed his arm where she had roughly grabbed it. "You don't seem like yourself today."

"You barely know me," Violet whispered. "And where is Kayla today, anyway?"

Jess reached out as if he was going to touch her shoulder, but stopped himself and retracted his arm. "We might not be close yet, but I want to get to know you. Or I did, before you started acting all weird this morning." He ran his hands through his curly brown hair. "Look, Kayla and I thought you could use some friends. We know what it's like to feel like an outcast. We thought you would be—"

"Be what? Grateful that you were nice enough to let me hang out with you?" Violet huffed and placed her hand on her hip, feeling feisty. She was sick of everyone's shit and felt herself nearing an explosion.

Jess vigorously shook his head and held out his hands placatingly. "No, it wasn't like that. You don't deserve everything that's happened to you since you moved here. No one deserves to be treated that way."

"Where's Kayla?" she asked again. She was almost always with Jess, so it was weird not to see her with him.

"She's playing hooky today."

*Figures she would be the type of person to skip school.*

They were in front of Violet's history classroom now. Violet gestured to the door. "This is my first class. See you at lunch?" she asked, softening her tone.

Jess nodded and left.

Violet inhaled, held her breath, counted to five, then tried to expel her anxiety as she slowly exhaled. Was she screwing things up with the only two people who had expressed an interest in being friends with her? Should she ignore their offer and continue going on the way she had been—being bullied ceaselessly and having no one to talk to—except her best friend, who was hundreds of miles away? That was no way to live. Maybe she was being unfair to Kayla and Jess. She decided to give them the benefit of the doubt. They couldn't be serious about that 'deep, dark desire for revenge' plot. Surely, it was all a joke. She would apologize to Jess at lunch. It would be easier to talk to him without Kayla around.

*Everything will be fine*, she tried to convince herself.

***

By the time lunch rolled around, Violet had rehearsed her apology to Jess numerous times. She didn't like going into situations like this unprepared. She preferred having a script for every situation. That way, she couldn't be surprised, no matter what happened.

This time, she didn't stress over her lunch choices. She didn't want to be the type of person who worried so much about what some guy thought. She chose spaghetti with a side of cheesy breadsticks because it sounded appetizing. Then she grabbed a Pepsi, thinking a burst of caffeine would boost her mood and energy. She saw Jess sitting at his usual table, so she sat in the seat next to him.

"Hey," she said shyly.

He seemed to study her. "Hi."

*Okay, he's definitely upset with me. It's fine. I prepared for this.*

"Jess—" she started her rehearsed apology, but he cut her off.

He held up his hand in a 'stop' gesture. "Hold on. Before you say anything, I wanted to apologize for... well, I guess assuming that Kayla and I are so great that you would want to be friends with us. But also, I'm sorry if we freaked you out when Kayla mentioned the 'dark desires' thing. She shouldn't have brought it up. And I don't know what she said to you when she drove you home last night, but hopefully it wasn't anything bad about me." Jess gave a nervous laugh at the end.

Violet leaned in closer to him. "I wanted to apologize, too. I'm sorry about how I acted this morning. The last few weeks have been really hard, and I've felt so alone." A few tears slipped down her face and she grew annoyed at herself for letting her emotions get out of control. She hoped Jess didn't notice and cleared her throat before she continued. "I'm glad you and Kayla offered to let me eat lunch with you and be a part of your group. For the record, Kayla didn't say anything bad about you. She mentioned you guys have been friends for a while. It made me miss Abby, my best friend back in Michigan."

"I understand. It must be tough starting over at a new school as a sophomore. At least I know most of the people here, even if they're all assholes." Jess smirked.

"Yeah. I can't take it any longer. I can't handle the bullying," Violet said in a defeated tone. Tear after tear spilled down her cheeks and betrayed her.

*Damn it. I didn't want to cry in front of him.*

Jess surprised her by wordlessly wrapping his arms around her in a tight embrace. At first, she was too shocked to react, but when he held onto her for more than a few seconds without letting go, she relaxed and wrapped her arms around his body gratefully. Just when Violet wondered if he would let go of her, he dropped his arms and stared into her eyes.

"Don't worry, Violet," he said with a fierce, burning look in his green eyes. "No one is going to hurt you like that again."

# Chapter 7: Before Jess

*September 3, 2019*

Violet idly wondered if she should tell her parents she was being bullied. She assumed they would be upset and want her to report Mallory's behavior, but Violet didn't think that was a good idea. She knew how these things worked. If she reported Mallory, her life would get worse. That would mean Mallory would have to be more creative about how she tortured her, and she didn't want another reason for Mallory to target her. It was already bad enough.

Her phone pinged with a text.

**Abby:** OMG I have news!
**Violet:** What's up?

**Abby:** Scott asked me out!

**Violet:** Seriously? When? How?

**Abby:** I'll tell you more later, but it was SO cute. Video chat tonight?

**Violet:** Sounds good. I'm happy for you, Abby!

Violet waited a minute, but didn't receive a response. She was happy for her friend, albeit a bit jealous. Scott was one of the most popular guys at their school. He was a junior and a star player for the basketball team. He was also incredibly cute. Violet hadn't known Abby was interested in him though, and the thought worried her. Since when did Abby want to date Scott? Why hadn't she told her sooner? It's not like he would have randomly asked her on a date, unless they had already been talking and hanging out. Something had to have led to that point. A sharp pang went through Violet's chest as she realized her best friend was moving on with her life without her. Soon, she would have no one.

\*\*\*

Violet sat in her Spanish class, failing to focus on Señora Iliza's lecture. Yet another boring monologue about the history of Spain. Like she cared. She had far more pressing things on her mind than historical Spanish wars. She didn't even know why Señora Iliza was talking about war. What did that have to do with learning how to speak Spanish?

She scribbled in her notebook, pretending to take notes, but mindlessly sketching instead. Mallory and Rose whispered in the row behind her, and she assumed they were talking shit about her. She didn't need to hear them to guess what they said.

Violet wondered for the hundredth time what made Mallory hate her so much. It had to have been more than Violet accidentally bumping into her. Had she unintentionally done something else to piss her off? What kind of person was so psychotic that they let an accident make them want to destroy someone's life and mercilessly bully them?

Thankfully, Spanish passed without incident, which had become rarer and rarer. Violet thought she was safe for the day when class ended, but Mallory and Rose cornered her in the hallway. Rose seemed to go along with whatever Mallory told her and was a faithful Mallory-worshipper, like most of the school.

As she trudged down the hall, someone grabbed Violet's shoulder from behind, pulling her back.

"Hey!" Violet protested as she stumbled and almost fell. "What do you want?" she asked in a quieter tone when she realized what had happened and who had grabbed her.

Both Mallory and Rose wore identical smirks. Mallory held her phone and appeared to be texting. After a few seconds of her long nails clacking on the phone screen and typing, she put her phone back in the front pocket of her backpack. Violet contemplated walking away. After all, Mallory hadn't said anything to her, and sticking around probably wouldn't end well. When she tried to escape, Rose roughly shoved her in Mallory's direction.

Mallory giggled.

"What's your problem?" Violet shouted. She may have normally been quiet, but they were being mean for no reason, and she wouldn't let this continue.

"My problem?" Mallory asked, raising a thin eyebrow. Her hand was on her hip, and she tapped her fingers against her hip. "I have no idea what you mean. You're the one who started this." She glared at Violet.

Rose showed her agreement by vigorously nodding at every word. Her dark, shoulder-length brown hair swished with every nod.

"All I did was bump into you on the first day of school. It's not like it was on purpose. Why are you out to get me?" Violet asked, grinding her teeth as she tried to show restraint. She didn't want to worsen the situation, but she was also sick of the way she was being treated like a pariah by everyone at school because Mallory had deemed her a target. No one would even talk to her.

Mallory smacked her sparkly, lip gloss-covered lips and smiled innocently. "Just wait, Violet. You think things are bad now? This is only the beginning. I'm going to ruin every single part of your life. No one will want to be friends with you when I'm done."

Violet snorted derisively. "I don't think you could make it any worse."

Mallory laughed. "Is that a challenge? Because I'll gladly make it my personal mission to make sure your life is a living hell."

Violet shrugged, attempting to appear nonchalant. She couldn't find the words to stick up for herself. Her frustration and anger boiled to a dangerous level, but she willed herself to stay calm. Or better yet, to walk away. But she couldn't make herself move. This time, instead of 'fight or flight,' she froze. Stuck in Mallory's path. Unable to escape. Helpless. Exactly what Mallory wanted.

Mallory took a step closer to Violet. Mallory was shorter than Violet, but she somehow loomed over her intimidatingly. "What's wrong? Cat got your tongue?" She snickered.

Rose snickered too and looked back and forth between Mallory and Violet, watching the scene play out.

Violet opened her mouth, hoping to come up with a witty retort on the fly, but Mallory countered before she said anything.

"You're such a dumbass you can't even stand up for yourself. How pathetic. No wonder no one likes you. The world would be better off without you. You should probably just run off and *kill yourself.*" Mallory spat each word viciously as she stepped closer to Violet.

This time Rose gasped, but she quickly tried to compose herself and hide her shock at Mallory's words.

"You bitch." Tears sprang to Violet's eyes as she finally snapped.

Mallory was right in front of her now, so close she couldn't resist the impulse to reach out and strike her across the cheek. The sound of the slap seemed to echo throughout the hall, despite the raucous students around them.

Several students held up their phones to record the incident. She barely had time to register Mallory staring at her in shock—and possibly a bit of admiration—before she took off running down the hallway. Violet didn't stop running until she had burst through the school's front doors. A secretary or teacher yelled at her to stop and said she couldn't leave, but she didn't care about anything besides getting away from Mallory.

When Violet reached the front courtyard, she collapsed onto one of the wooden benches engraved with the name of a wealthy family who had donated money to the high school. She didn't have time to think about the consequences or what she should do next before she saw the principal headed her way.

# Chapter 8:
# After Jess

*September 18, 2019*

The bell rang, signaling the end of the school day. Violet anxiously went to her locker to grab her other textbooks and her thin coat. A light coat was perfectly fine for the middle of September in Asheville, although she knew she would need a warmer coat for the winter. North Carolina locals had warned her that the winters could be fierce, but she doubted it would be anything like a Michigan winter. She was meeting Jess and Kayla in the parking lot, but this time, instead of going to Jess's parents' coffee shop, they were going somewhere more private where they could talk. Jess promised they would tell her more about their plans.

When she found Kayla's Corolla in the parking lot, Kayla and Jess were both already there.

"Hop in," Kayla said, waving Violet over. "I snuck out, so I don't want to be gone super long."

Violet stared at her quizzically. "You snuck out? But Jess said you played hooky today. Why did you have to sneak out? Is something wrong?"

Kayla shot a look at Jess—was she mad at him? Why?

Jess's gaze dropped, and he scuffed his shoe on the pavement. "Just get in the car," he said to Violet.

Violet complied, but she was still bewildered. Her unanswered questions piled up, and she wondered again what she was getting into. Was it worth the risk? Then again, what did she have to lose at this point?

Kayla turned on the same classic rock as last time, which was so loud Violet thought her eardrums would burst. No one spoke until Kayla stopped the car at a park and turned off the music. The sudden silence invaded her ears.

"Are you getting out or what?" Kayla asked as she and Jess stood outside the car, waiting for Violet.

"Yeah, sorry. Just spacing out. Why are we here?" Violet asked as she surveyed the area. She opted to leave her backpack in the car and joined them outside.

It was a dingy-looking park. There weren't any other cars in the parking lot and it was devoid of people, except for them. The park didn't have much going for it: a few swings, a slide that looked like it would fall apart if anyone over twenty pounds went down it, and further beyond, there was an open field that led to the woods. She wondered why they were there and guessed it wasn't exactly a popular hangout spot. Most parents probably preferred to take their kids to the nicer parks that were safe and renovated, not places like this in the middle of nowhere that were dangerous and most likely full of diseases.

"Come on, we're going this way." Jess beckoned for Violet to follow him and Kayla.

They headed toward the open field. Violet hoped they weren't going into the woods. It looked creepy, like something straight out of a horror movie, even though the sun still shone brightly. She noted again that they were the only ones at the park. And they were definitely going into the woods.

"Where are we going?" Violet hesitated at the edge of the trees. She wasn't sure she wanted to follow Jess and Kayla if she didn't know what was going on or where they were headed.

*What if this was part of their plan? What if they wanted to hurt her? Or worse?*

"We have a secret spot in the woods for when we want to talk without anyone overhearing us. No one else comes here," Jess explained cryptically.

*Well, great. That makes me feel way better.*

But she continued to follow Jess and Kayla, despite her trepidation. Everything had already been taken from her. It couldn't possibly get worse. Besides, if something happened to her, would that be so bad?

When they were in the woods, they didn't stop until they reached a cluster of trees that formed an archway.

"We call it Aragog's lair." Jess laughed, clearly amused with himself.

"Clever," Violet said with a smile, appreciating the *Harry Potter* reference.

Kayla entered the lair first, then Jess went after her, leaving Violet no choice but to follow. They sat only a few feet into the lair, so it wasn't very dark. Sunlight peeked through the tree branches, so they could still see each other, which made Violet slightly less apprehensive. At least she would see it and have a warning if someone came after her. She could only imagine the creeps who hung out at a park like this.

"You might wonder why we insist on all this secrecy," Kayla started.

"Yeah, kinda," Violet replied.

Jess brushed his curly brown hair out of his eyes and glanced at Kayla as if asking for permission. Kayla nodded.

Violet noticed Jess pull a silver lighter out of his pocket and flick it so that a flame glowed in front of his face. "So, it started last year. I was dating a girl that I was crazy about. We went through a very public break-up—"

"With who?" Violet couldn't stop herself from asking. Part of it was morbid curiosity and the other part was jealousy of whoever had been fortunate enough to date him.

Jess's lips turned down. He flicked the lighter off again. He clearly didn't like reliving his pain. Or maybe he wasn't completely over the girl yet? She didn't know him well enough to know for sure.

"It doesn't matter who it was," he insisted. "Around the same time I was dealing with my break-up, Kayla was also dealing with something difficult." Jess paused, smiled at Kayla sympathetically, and resumed his explanation. "We were both in a terrible place and leaned on each other for support—"

"Okay, yeah, enough about what happened to us," Kayla snapped impatiently, interrupting Jess. "You're drawing this out. She doesn't need to know all the gory details of what we both went through." Kayla turned to Violet. "Use your imagination, but trust me when I tell you, it wasn't pretty." Kayla's face looked grim.

Violet wondered how bad it was. Worse than a terrible public break-up? Worse than being bullied? It must be something awful to have shaken her like that. Kayla had mentioned her mom's boyfriend before, so Violet could only imagine what terrible thing Kayla had endured. She seemed so tough and almost untouchable. She didn't strike Violet as the type of girl who was shaken easily.

"So, you both had a bad year. What does that have to do with the 'deep, dark desires' thing you keep mentioning?"

Kayla and Jess exchanged a look that Violet couldn't interpret. It was the look of two people who were close enough that they could communicate without words. Like the relationship she used to have with Abby. Did Kayla and Jess regret involving her now? And what was the secret they were keeping from her?

The longer Violet waited for an answer to her question, the more annoyed she became. She wasn't sure why she had followed two classmates she barely knew into this dark, creepy lair in the woods where there were no other people around and no witnesses if something happened. No one even knew she was there. This time, she had neglected to text her dad and let him know where she was going.

What had she been thinking? Was she really that desperate for friends that she was willing to risk her life? Apparently.

Jess cleared his throat and scooted closer to Violet. He placed his hand on her knee. Violet glanced at his hand as her knee burned like it was on fire from his touch.

"Well, are you going to tell me what your plan is?" Violet asked with more confidence than she felt, trying to ignore Jess's hand still on her knee.

"Revenge," Kayla replied with a sinister smile that appeared even creepier in the encroaching darkness. "We're going to get revenge on everyone who wronged us, Violet."

# Chapter 9:
# Before Jess

*September 3, 2019*

Principal Collins personally escorted Violet to his office. Principal Collins had a bushy mustache and was balding. He also had a penchant for wearing designer suits, despite his not exactly prestigious title as high school principal. Clearly, he was a man who aspired to greater things.

She sat across from him in a cushioned chair, with his impressive executive-looking wooden desk in between them. He stared at her and kept licking his lips nervously, as if he was trying to figure out how to approach the situation. The incident had literally just happened, so clearly, someone had told him immediately. It was her luck that she couldn't get away with the one slip up she made.

"Violet," he started, licking his lips yet again. "Do you know why you're in here today?"

*What a stupid question*, she thought, and resisted the urge to roll her eyes. She needed to be careful how she responded.

"Yes," Violet said, not wanting to volunteer any unnecessary information. She didn't know how much Principal Collins had heard about the situation yet, and she didn't want to make things worse for herself.

Principal Collins picked up the water bottle on his desk and took a large gulp of water. "You're a new student," he said as he looked at the file on his desk, which must have contained her school records.

"Yes."

"Have you made many friends in Asheville? Are you involved in any sports or extracurricular activities?"

Violet contemplated the question. Should she be honest? She didn't have any friends, but admitting that made her sound pathetic. A few weeks had passed since the school year had started. She was probably the only one at the high school with no friends. He had asked what activities she was involved in, but the answer was none. Even though Violet had tried out for the dance team, she hadn't made the cut, so she didn't want to reveal that either.

Violet shrugged her shoulders in a noncommittal answer.

Principal Collins rubbed his balding head. "Not very talkative, are you?" he said with a chuckle.

Violet bit her lip and didn't reply.

Principal Collins leaned forward, folding his hands on the desk. "Well, let's get down to it, then. As I'm sure you can imagine, I'm a busy man. I don't like being bothered by things like this, but it seemed necessary for me to intervene. So, tell me. What happened earlier?"

"Mallory and Rose confronted me in the hallway. Mallory has been tormenting me for weeks. She's been bullying me since the first day of school and—"

"Whoa there." Principal Collins held his hand out in front of him. "Bullying is a serious accusation. We don't tolerate that sort of behavior here." He frowned as he stroked his bushy mustache. "Ms. McKenzie is a popular student. She gets good grades and has lots of friends. I can't see her being the type of person to bully someone. Are you sure you didn't misinterpret the situation? Maybe you're a bit—" He paused before finishing the sentence. "Sensitive?"

Violet fumed and her face turned red in anger. "Principal Collins, in the past few weeks, Mallory has belittled me, teased me, harassed me during Spanish class—which we unfortunately have together— and she has done everything she can to make my life a living hell!"

"Okay, Ms. Hale, I don't allow profanity in my office, but I get your point. Do you have any proof of this so-called bullying?"

Violet stared at him, aghast at his response. "Proof?"

"Yes, can any witnesses attest to what happened? Did anyone see one of these incidents when Ms. McKenzie bullied you? Several students came forward today with videos of you slapping her, so I'm inclined to believe that you were the instigator in this situation. Ms. McKenzie is currently sitting in the nurse's office, waiting to find out if there is serious damage to her face." He shook his head slowly, as if it was the saddest thing he had ever heard.

Violet almost laughed. All she had done was slap her. It's not like she was a trained fighter. She hadn't even slapped her that hard.

Although, part of her did hope there was permanent damage to Mallory's pretty little face.

"Principal Collins…" She tried to find the right words to convince him that her only mistake was slapping Mallory. "Mallory provoked me. She was trying to get a reaction out of me, and I know I didn't react how I should have, but she made me do it."

Principal Collins shook his head disapprovingly. "I'm sorry, Ms. Hale, but that doesn't line up with what Ms. McKenzie told me. I can't let students at my school get away with this type of behavior. As far as I can tell, you never had disciplinary issues at your previous school, so you'll get off lightly this time. You'll be suspended for three days. I'll also be calling your parents to notify them about the situation. Take the time away from the school to consider the effects of what you did. I don't know what your previous high school was like in Michigan, but we don't tolerate physical abuse or any sort of abuse here. Rest assured, Ms. Hale, step out of line again, and I will expel you."

"But, Principal Collins, that's not fa—"

"Many things in life aren't fair. It's best you learn that while you're young. It's difficult to change the older you get, so I hope you take the suspension to heart and something good comes out of this terrible situation." He rubbed his bald head again and muttered, "It doesn't make the school look good."

"Is that it?" Violet rose from her chair with her fists clenched.

Principal Collins nodded. "Yes, you can wait in the main office. I'll call your parents and tell them what happened. They can come pick you up."

Violet didn't deem that worthy of a response, so she grabbed her backpack and stalked to the main office, where she plopped down in another chair and wondered how everything had gotten so messed up. She didn't think things could get worse. But she was wrong. Her parents were going to kill her.

The Quiet Girl

# Chapter 10: After Jess

*September 18, 2019*

After the weird hangout with Kayla and Jess, Violet sat at home in her bedroom, definitely not working on her homework. Despite her trepidation at whatever secrets Jess and Kayla weren't telling her—there was clearly more to it than what they admitted to her earlier—she was excited at the prospect of having friends to text again. Abby hadn't texted her in days, and she assumed it was because of her new boyfriend, Scott, taking up her free time. She was too busy to check on her dear friend Violet.

Violet's phone glowed with a new text message. It's not like she was getting any homework done, so she didn't feel too guilty about checking her phone. She already had Kayla's phone number and Jess had shared his shortly after, so she assumed it was one of them.

**Jess:** Hey.
**Violet:** Hey.

Her heart raced as she typed her response. Did she respond too fast? Was it dumb that she copied his text? Should she have said something else? What did he want? Three dots appeared that meant he was typing.

**Jess:** Do you want to go to Big Beanz with me tomorrow? Kayla has a dentist appointment after school, so it will just be the two of us. My mom can pick us up from school.
**Violet:** Sure, that would be great!
**Jess:** Can't wait. :)
**Violet:** Me too. :)

Violet set down her phone, feeling like she had just run three miles. She wished it was easier for her to talk to boys. Or to anyone. It was part of the struggle of her anxiety. Her energy drained if she was around people for too long, and she enjoyed her alone time. Of course, Jess was someone she wanted to be around, so it differed from usual. But still, how could she possibly get through a date with him without making a fool of herself? She didn't want to screw it up.

She laid back against her pile of fuzzy pillows and wondered what her date with Jess would be like. *Wait. It was a date, wasn't it?*

Violet jumped up from her bed, sending several pillows to the floor, and stomped over to her closet. She threw the double doors open, rummaging through the hangers and muttering to herself. She stood in the middle of her walk-in closet on the verge of losing her sanity when Emilia flung open her bedroom door.

Emilia stood in the doorway with her hands on her hips. "What are you doing, Vi? I can't concentrate on my algebra homework with all the noise you're making." She entered Violet's bedroom without an invitation and sauntered over to the closet. "You need an outfit for something?"

Violet wearily nodded. Her sister was probably the best person to help her, even if she was two years younger. She knew what guys liked. She was only thirteen and already had guys falling all over themselves to date her. "I think I… I have a date tomorrow after school."

Emilia gasped and held her hand to her heart dramatically. "Oh my God, I need to live vicariously through you! It's so stupid that Mom and Dad won't let me date until high school." She rolled her eyes and started flipping through the hangers in Violet's closet. "Maybe you should borrow one of my outfits?" she suggested as she shoved aside most of Violet's wardrobe. "Where's the date?"

"I'm not sure if it's a date. He texted me and asked if I wanted to go to his parents' coffee shop with him tomorrow." Violet groaned. "I can't do this."

"Yes, you can. What's his name? And a coffee shop? So, nothing too fancy then…" Emilia tapped her finger on her chin as she thought.

"His name is Jess. His parents own Big Beanz Coffee in downtown Asheville."

"Wait, *that* Jess?" Emilia's eyes widened. "Nice. He's really cute."

"Hold on, how do *you* know Jess?"

Emilia shrugged nonchalantly. "I've gone to Big Beanz with some friends a few times. Mom and Dad let me hang out there because they think I can't get into any trouble at a coffee shop." She gave a mischievous grin that suggested their parents were wrong.

Violet anxiously ran her fingers through her hair and paced. "Do you think jeans and a cute top would be all right? I have to wear it to school all day and probably won't have time to change before the date."

Emilia pulled a flouncy, short-sleeved maroon blouse off a hanger in the closet and proceeded over to Violet's dresser, where she snatched up a pair of skinny, dark wash jeans from the bottom drawer. "These are the jeans that your butt looks good in, right?"

Violet stared at her sister, unsure how to react to that statement. "Uh—"

"Just put this on and show me what it looks like together." Emilia went over to Violet's bed, crossed her legs and made herself comfortable, and waited for Violet to change.

After a few minutes, Violet turned to face her sister. "I'm not sure about this." She tugged on the jeans uncomfortably as she looked down at them. "I haven't worn these jeans in a while. I think they're too tight."

Emilia flipped back her blonde locks dramatically. "That's the point, Vi."

"Okay, if you're sure."

"Yup, wear that tomorrow, and then report back to me with an update when you get home."

"You make this sound like it's some sort of mission."

Emilia smiled innocently. "Well, it kind of is. Just try not to stress about it too much. He clearly likes you if he asked you out for coffee. And don't forget to have fun."

"Right."

"Relax, you'll be fine. It's only a date."

"I hope so," Violet replied, biting her lip so hard she tasted blood. She needed to chill.

***

*September 19, 2019*

The next day was uneventful until Violet met Jess in front of the school, when the last class had ended for the day. She was anxious about his mom driving them to the coffee shop because that forced her to make awkward small talk with the mom of the boy she liked. And she still wasn't sure if it was a date.

When she exited the school, the sun shone brightly, despite the slight chill in the air. It was nearly October, and the cold weather would soon settle into Asheville for the next few months. Violet wished she had worn a jacket, but she didn't want to cover up her carefully selected outfit. Jess stood on the sidewalk, shielding his eyes from the bright sunlight with his hand. He smiled when he saw her.

"Hey." Jess surprised her by wrapping his arms around her in a hug.

Violet hugged him back, forgetting her anxiety for the moment and savoring the feeling of his body close to hers.

"Ready?" he asked as he stepped back and ended the hug.

Violet nodded. Jess grabbed her hand and tugged her to the visitor's parking lot where his mom, Jasmine, waited in her black, five-passenger SUV. Jasmine waved cheerfully when they approached the car. Jess opened the car door for Violet and gestured for her to enter the car, then he slid into the backseat and sat next to Violet.

"Hi, Mom," Jess said.

"Hi, thanks for picking us up," Violet said politely.

"Oh, no problem. Jess's dad can hold down the fort for a bit," his mom replied with a slight laugh. "So, how was school?"

"Fine," Jess responded.

Violet nodded in agreement.

"That's good. What is it that your parents do, Violet?" Jasmine asked.

Jess groaned obnoxiously. "Mom, I told you not to interrogate the girl I like!"

Violet's face flushed at Jess's admission. She glanced at him, and he smiled sheepishly.

Jasmine chuckled. "Oh, I just want to get to know her, Jess! You're bringing her to my coffee shop, after all. Besides, if you like her, then she must be special. You haven't dated anyone since—"

"Oh. My. God," Jess loudly interrupted. "Are you going to bring up literally everything I asked you not to?"

"Well, I don't see why you wouldn't want Violet to know, but I'll respect your wishes," Jasmine said primly. "Is there any topic I'm allowed to discuss during this drive?"

"I don't know. Something generic, like the weather or whatever. Next thing I know, you'll be pulling out my baby pictures or those home videos Dad took when I was little," Jess said sarcastically.

"Oh! I'm sure Violet would love to see those. I should have planned for that," Jasmine retorted.

Jess was about to protest, but Jasmine shot him a look. "I was kidding, Jess. Calm down. You're going to scare her off."

Violet let a giggle escape from her mouth. "Sorry," she immediately said when she saw Jess's expression. "It was funny."

Jess sighed. "What do your parents do?"

Violet looked at him, confused by his question. She remembered telling him about her parent's jobs the first time they went to Big Beanz together. Maybe he had forgotten. Or was he just asking for his mom's sake? "My mom is a marketing manager. We moved here because of her job. The company offered her a big promotion if she agreed to move. My dad is a dentist."

Jasmine smiled. "We always need more dentists. And... a marketing manager? That sounds interesting."

"Yeah, her job has changed a lot since the rise in social media use. My mom always says advertising isn't like it used to be, but she's great at her job."

"Maybe she can help us with marketing for the coffee shop," Jasmine said thoughtfully.

Violet hesitated, not wanting to volunteer her mom to do something for free and knowing her mom didn't have time for things like that.

Thankfully, Jess cut in. "Violet's mom is probably too busy to help."

"Of course, just an idea, dear. Do you have any siblings, Violet?"

"Yeah, my sister Emilia is thirteen and my brother Glenn is seventeen."

"Jess is an only child," Jasmine responded before Jess could form a response.

"Do I get to be a part of this conversation?" Jess asked irritably, crossing his arms over his chest.

After what felt like the longest car ride of Violet's life, Jasmine pulled the car into the parking lot of Big Beanz Coffee. Violet opened the door, grateful for a reprieve from the questions about her personal life and family.

"Here we are!" Jasmine announced, although Violet had already jumped out of the car the second it stopped moving.

Jess soon followed her out of the car. "Come on, let's get away while we still can," Jess whispered, grabbing Violet's hand and pulling her into the coffee shop.

"I heard that, Jess!" Jasmine yelled as she clicked the key fob to lock the car and slammed the driver's side door.

Jess's eyes widened—whether in fear of his mom or the fact that he was holding her hand, Violet wasn't sure—either way, he pulled her along faster.

They entered the coffee shop hand-in-hand. Jess led her to the same table they had sat at before, but it looked completely different from last time. Before, the table had been empty. Now a white linen tablecloth covered the rough wooden surface. Shimmery silver napkins were folded into triangles in front of two chairs, and there was a clear vase with a single purple chrysanthemum inside it in the middle of the table.

Jess pulled out a chair for Violet.

She sat in the chair and smiled up at him. "The flower is beautiful," she said, not missing the irony of a purple flower when her name was Violet. She pulled the vase toward her to sniff the flower and inspected it more closely.

Jess returned the smile and sat down across from her. "I'm glad you like it. I wanted our first date to be special."

Violet laughed, and Jess stared at her.

"What?" he asked, with a confused look.

"I wasn't sure if this was a date. Or if you liked me," Violet said shyly.

"Honestly, I wasn't sure if you liked me, either. You gave me mixed signals. Sorry, I thought I was clear about my intentions."

"What exactly are your intentions with me?" Violet teased, gazing into his sparkling green eyes.

Jess glanced around the coffee shop. "I don't want to say it out loud in case one of my parents is listening," he replied and winked at her.

Violet's stomach somersaulted, and she became even more nervous than she had been. She smiled with her lips pressed together and folded her hands in her lap.

"Did I mention how pretty you are?" Jess grinned.

"No, but thank you."

"What? You aren't going to tell me I'm pretty too?" Jess asked, batting his eyelashes at her jokingly.

Violet shook her head and couldn't keep the smile off her face. Jess was ridiculous. He was one of the hottest guys at their school. "You don't need me to tell you that."

"Still. It's nice to hear. Guys like being told they look good too, you know."

"Hmm. I guess so." She tried not to fidget with her hands in her lap.

"You don't believe me?"

"No, I just think you like being complimented," she said with a knowing smirk.

"Our dinner should be served soon," Jess told her, changing the subject.

"Dinner? It's like 4 p.m." Violet glanced at the time on her phone.

"Yeah, well, I'm working with what I've got. The coffee shop isn't open super late on weeknights, so an early dinner made sense."

"Then why did you ask me out on a weeknight?"

"Because I didn't want to wait until the weekend. Is that okay?" Jess responded with another dazzling smile.

Violet shrugged. *Of course it's okay*, she wanted to say, but she clammed up in front of him again. Sometimes she could pretend to be outgoing and do things like talk to cute guys without becoming tongue-tied. But other times, she had no clue what to talk about and decided not saying anything was safer.

Jess drummed his fingers on the table. Was he impatient about waiting to eat? Did he regret asking her out? Was he annoyed that she was so quiet? What was going through his mind?

Jess suddenly stopped drumming and tugged at the collar of his short-sleeve polo shirt. He stared at her as if he was working up the courage to say something. "Sorry if I'm not great at the whole dating thing. It's been a while."

"It's fine. I mean—you're fine. I'm the awkward one," Violet replied with a nervous laugh.

"No, you're not. I can tell how much you think things through before you talk. Not many people care that much about what they say. I appreciate how thoughtful you are."

"Oh, thanks." Violet wasn't sure how to interpret his comment. Was that a compliment?

Jess continued as if Violet hadn't said anything, "Besides, getting to know you the past few days, I've felt this connection between us and I—Well, I really like you, Violet."

She smiled back. Since the date had started, she couldn't stop smiling. She had worried for no reason. He liked her, and that was all that mattered. She couldn't remember the last time she felt this way. "I like you too."

"I wish you were always smiling like that," he told her as he gazed deeply into her eyes.

Violet laughed in an awkward attempt to break the sexual tension, but it had the opposite effect.

"Can I kiss you?" he asked softly.

Violet's heart thudded like someone banging on a drum set, and she nodded.

Jess leaned across the table, closing the distance between them, so she felt the full impact of his gorgeous green eyes. Violet leaned in to meet him when the door to the back room swung open, and they both backed away from each other, leaning back in their chairs, as if they hadn't been about to kiss.

A man with Jess's curly brown hair came over to their table, carrying a tray full of food. "Hey, I'm Christopher Woodfield, Jess's dad. Nice to meet you, Violet. Jess has told me a lot about you."

Violet reached out her hand, then realized she couldn't shake his hand because he was still holding the full tray with both hands. "Nice to meet you, too."

"I hope you like pizza," Christopher said as he beamed at her. He set down the plates on their table.

One plate had a pepperoni pizza on it. The second plate had a plain cheese pizza with no discernible toppings that Violet could see. The third plate had garlic bread sticks and a dish of marinara sauce. Christopher also set down two plates, silverware, and water glasses.

"Thank you for dinner," Violet said politely.

"Yup, thanks, Dad," Jess said with a meaningful look at Christopher that Violet assumed meant 'get out of here.'

"I'll just be getting out of your hair then. Enjoy," Christopher said with a slight wave and a smile as he picked up the tray and headed back to the kitchen.

Violet stared at the food, not wanting to be the first one to eat, and her stomach grumbled loudly.

"Hungry?" Jess asked with a chuckle.

*Ugh, so embarrassing*, she thought. "Yeah, a little. What kind of pizza is it?"

"That one's pepperoni. And the other one is cheese," Jess responded, pointing at the pizzas. "I wasn't sure if you were a vegetarian, so I figured cheese was a safe back-up."

"I'm not, but I appreciate the thought." She grabbed a slice of pepperoni and took a careful bite. She tried not to think about the fact that she had definitely eaten chicken nuggets, pepperoni pizza, and a meatball sub in front of him during lunch the past few days. Was he just forgetful, or was he not paying attention to anything she said and did?

The pizza was fresh out of the oven, and the sauce and melted cheese immediately burned her tongue. "Mmm, this pizza's good," she said, embarrassed, as she dropped the steaming slice onto the plate.

"Yeah, my dad makes the best homemade pizza. Doesn't compare to any pizza chains around here."

"Oh my God, it's homemade?"

Jess's eyes widened. "Uh. Yeah?"

"Wow. Neither of my parents can cook like that. We usually eat takeout for dinner or mac and cheese."

Jess beamed proudly. "He cooks everything for the coffee shop. But he made the pizza especially for us tonight."

"I was wondering about that. I didn't think a coffee shop would serve pizza."

"Yeah, that would be kinda weird." Jess had already polished off one piece of pizza and was well into the second slice.

Violet grabbed a bread stick, broke off a piece, and dipped it into the marinara sauce. "Your mom mentioned you're an only child? What's that like?"

Jess chewed while he pondered his words. "It's... hard sometimes. All of my parent's attention is on me, so I feel a lot of pressure to be perfect." He lowered his voice. "And they wanted another kid, but my mom had a miscarriage, so I don't know if they gave up after that or decided I was enough."

"I'm sure that was hard," Violet replied, reaching across the table boldly to hold Jess's hand in hers. They seemed to fit together perfectly; her tiny hand enclosed in his normal-sized one. "And I think you're more than enough."

Violet wondered if he would try to kiss her again, but he didn't. He asked her about her classes, Michigan and how different it was there, her siblings, her hobbies, and her favorite bands. By the end of their first date, Jess knew all the basic aspects of her life and her likes and dislikes. But she realized he had barely revealed anything about himself. Why was that? And why did she feel like he was hiding something regarding whoever he had dated last year? Whatever it was, she was intent on figuring it out.

# Chapter 11:
# Before Jess

*September 4, 2019*

While Violet endured being suspended from school for three days, she had too much time to think. Mostly unhappy thoughts about how her life sucked, and she wanted to move back to Michigan. Soon, she was supposed to have a video chat with Abby. Violet planned to ask if her parents would let her live with them while she finished high school. She wasn't sure if her parents would go for the idea, let alone Abby's parents, but she had to try. She couldn't stay here and continue her life the way it was going. Abby would understand. She would help her. That's what best friends were supposed to do.

Her cell phone dinged several times with the announcement of a video chat request. She clicked ACCEPT, and the brightly smiling face of her best friend appeared onscreen. Her long blonde hair was piled in a messy bun on top of her head, and she had lined her blue eyes with eyeliner and mascara.

Violet glanced at her appearance in the mirror across from her bed and clenched her teeth together. No one had seen her besides her family for several days, so she had given up on wearing makeup or putting much effort into her appearance. As long as she was home, it didn't matter. She wasn't trying to impress anyone. But after seeing how cute Abby looked, she felt like a slob.

"Hey, Abby! You look good." Violet plastered a smile on her face.

Abby scoffed and looked down at her baggy sweatshirt. Did that say Highland Horses? Was she wearing one of Scott's sweatshirts?

"I do not," Abby replied flippantly, tousling her messy bun.

"Is that Scott's sweatshirt?"

Abby smiled hugely. "It might be," she said with a giggle.

Violet shook her head with a small smile. "Are you two officially dating now?"

Abby suddenly pouted. "Not yet, but I'm sure he'll ask me to be his girlfriend soon."

Violet didn't say anything for a moment as she pondered how to approach the subject.

"Oh yeah, I almost forgot to tell you. I saw Charlie the other day," Abby said tentatively.

Violet tried to still her suddenly pounding heart. "Oh, that's nice," she said, trying to appear carefree and casual. "How's he doing?"

Abby grinned and spilled the gossip. "He asked how you were doing, what you've been up to. He's still crazy about you. Since you moved, he hasn't dated anyone."

Violet smiled as she reminisced about her past. It felt good to be wanted, even if she felt bad for her ex-boyfriend. At first, she had been heartbroken about the situation, making moving even worse. "He was always so sweet. Breaking up was for the best, though. There's no way we could have made long-distance work."

"Yeah, plus I'm sure there are tons of sweet, cute Southern gentlemen in Asheville!" Abby squealed.

Violet rolled her eyes. "If you know of any, send them my way."

The two friends lapsed into a comfortable quiet for a few seconds until Abby broke the silence. She was never good at sitting quietly. "So, how's Asheville? Any better?"

"Well, that's actually what I wanted to talk to you about."

Abby nodded encouragingly.

"I got suspended for slapping Mallory."

Abby yelped and disappeared for a moment. The view shifted to what Violet assumed was her bedroom carpet. *She must have dropped her phone.*

"O.M.G. What happened, Violet?" Abby asked as she adjusted her phone's camera and reappeared on-screen a few seconds later.

"She was trying to provoke me. She confronted me in the hallway yesterday, and I couldn't take it any longer. You should have heard the things she said to me—" Violet trailed off, not wanting to relive the horrible day. "There were a bunch of other students in the hallway, so other people witnessed it and recorded videos on their phones. Someone must have told the principal. I tried explaining what happened, but he wouldn't listen to me. My parents don't even believe me," Violet said with a loud sigh.

"Wow, I'm so sorry. I can't believe you got suspended, and it wasn't your fault! Mallory sounds like a psycho. What are you going to do?"

"I don't know. I had an idea, but I need your help."

"Of course! Whatever you need. You know I'm always here for you," Abby reassured her.

Violet smiled, relieved that Abby had agreed to help her so easily. "Oh, thank God. I was worried you would say no."

Abby's face scrunched up in confusion. "Wait, what's your idea? What did I just agree to?"

Violet took a deep breath and exhaled loudly. "I'm miserable here. I can't go on like this. At school, I'm bullied every day. I don't have any friends or anyone to talk to. So, I was wondering if… if you could talk to your parents and see if they would let me move in with you. Moving back to Michigan seems like the best solut—"

Abby winced. "Sorry, Vi. I don't think that's possible."

Violet scoffed and pretended that Abby's reaction didn't hurt her. She had immediately shot down her idea before she even finished explaining it. "Can't we at least talk about it?"

"My parents won't go for that. Especially if your parents want you to stay there."

"Yeah, but I thought if I told you my plan and you got your parent's permission first, then my parents would be more likely to agree. If they knew your parents were already on board with it, it would be easier to convince them it was a good idea. They don't care about what's going on at school. They're mad that I got suspended."

Abby chewed on her lip. "I mean—can you blame them for being upset? I understand why you did it, but you slapped another student in the middle of the hallway with witnesses. Did you think you were going to get away with it?"

"Mallory provoked me on purpose! She was trying to get me in trouble. She probably planned it all out with her friend Rose," Violet protested, moving her phone around wildly as she spoke.

"Even if she did, you can't prove anything, right? I really am sorry, Violet. Is there something else I can do?" Abby asked, her blue eyes sympathetic.

"No, it's fine. I'll continue suffering alone like I have been for the past month since I moved. You've been so obsessed with Scott that you haven't bothered to see how I'm doing. Not like you care that I'm going through the hardest thing I've ever endured. So much for being best friends. I guess we aren't anymore. You know I would do anything for you, but I guess you don't feel the same," Violet ranted, ending the video call after her outburst. She didn't want to stick around to see Abby's reaction.

Violet tossed her phone aside, not bothering to check where it landed, even if it was on the faux hardwood floor that might damage it. She didn't care. What was the point of having a phone if she had no one to talk to? She slumped down on her bed, chucking the stupid pillows onto the floor and curling up under the covers. She probably had homework she could work on, but she didn't care about that either. What was the point of anything? A shudder erupted throughout her body and she tried to maintain her self-control, but in the end, she lost, and sobs exploded from her mouth. Violet closed her eyes as she cried, deciding she couldn't hold it in any longer.

Her bedroom door opened, and she opened her eyes to see who was there. A dark blonde ponytail popped around the doorway. Emilia wordlessly shut the door, walked over to Violet's bed, and curled up under the covers with her, wrapping her into her tiny arms. Nothing needed to be said.

# Chapter 12:
# After Jess

*September 30, 2019*

The next week and a half passed quickly after Violet's first date with Jess. For the first time since she had moved to Asheville, her life felt normal. Most days, she was happy. She fell into a routine with Jess and Kayla. Every day, they met in the courtyard before their first class. During their lunch period, they ate together, and they always met up after school. Sometimes Jess walked her to her classes. Most afternoons, Kayla drove them all to Big Beanz, where they hung out, drank iced coffee, and ate snacks prepared by Jess's dad. The trio joked around and acted like they were regular teenagers. But they weren't. Whenever Violet was with them, she felt darkness simmering under the surface of their conversations. She wondered what it would take to make it spill over.

As October approached, the leaves changed colors and the mountainous area became chilly. Violet owned an extensive fall and winter wardrobe since she grew up in Michigan, so she was fine with the weather, and she welcomed the cold. She couldn't stand the heat and was thankful the sweltering summer seemed to be over at last.

Jess still hadn't told her anything about his dating history. Violet was determined to find out who Jess dated and why it was such a big secret. She knew the right way to do it was to get to know him better and eventually bring it up. He needed to trust her first. Briefly, she contemplated begging Kayla to spill the secret, but she assumed Jess would be mad at Violet for not asking him directly, and he would also be mad at Kayla for telling her.

The only problem was that Violet and Jess hadn't been alone together since their first date. Kayla was always with them. She seemed to pop up whenever Violet wanted to talk to Jess privately. She wondered if Kayla did it on purpose or if it was a crazy coincidence that she kept interrupting them and disturbing their alone time.

Besides the fact that Violet wanted to talk to Jess alone, she also wanted to be alone with him for other reasons, and she had thought Jess felt the same way, but now she wasn't sure. If he wanted to kiss her, why didn't he? Ever since their first date, he hadn't tried to kiss her again. It was maddening, and Violet wasn't brave enough to bring it up to him.

Before school started one day, she waited in the outdoor courtyard for Jess and Kayla, like usual. She sat on a bench, reading a book from the library. When she looked up and spotted her friends coming toward her, she placed a bookmark in the book and put the book in her backpack. She sat up straighter against the back of the wooden bench and waited for them to reach her. This was her chance.

"Hey," Jess said, bending down to give her a hug while she remained seated.

Violet smiled and hugged him back. "Hey."

Kayla rolled her eyes playfully. "Yeah, yeah, you guys are adorable. Can we go inside? It's fucking freezing out here."

Violet laughed. "I don't mind the cold," she said, staring up at Jess and hoping he took the hint.

"Why don't you go inside, and we'll catch up with you in a few minutes?" Jess suggested to Kayla, widening his eyes meaningfully.

"I get it. You want to be alone with her. You can just tell me that, Jess." Kayla hoisted her backpack on her shoulder and headed toward the school's main entrance. "Use a condom!" she yelled, waving as she left.

Violet's cheeks grew warm as several students passing by turned to look at them and snickered.

"She was just messing around," Jess said with a smirk as he stood over Violet and leaned forward, placing his hands on either side of her on the top rail of the bench.

Violet's breathing became unsteady as Jess moved closer. Just when she wondered if she should grab him by his T-shirt and kiss him first, he closed the distance and gently pressed his lips against hers for a few seconds. She kissed him back, and he put his icy hand on her flushed cheek as he kissed her again. He leaned back slightly, gazing at her to gauge her reaction.

"*Finally*," Violet said, at first not realizing she said it out loud.

Jess looked at her for a few seconds before he burst out laughing and joined her on the bench. "You were waiting for me to kiss you, huh?"

"Um. Yeah."

Jess's cheeks were pink. Violet wasn't sure if it was from the cold or from embarrassment. "Sorry. It was hard to find the right time because Kayla was always around."

"I know. I've been wanting to ask you something. So, now that we're finally alone—"

"Uh, now that we're alone, there are plenty of other things I would rather do than talk," Jess said with a mischievous grin.

Violet sighed in annoyance. "We'll have time for that at some point, but this is important."

Jess must have realized how serious she was because his smile vanished, and he turned to face her fully. He grabbed one of her chilled hands and warmed it between his. "Okay. What's up?"

"Jess, I know you went through a traumatic break-up last year, and I wondered—"

Jess dropped her hand and leaned back against the bench. "Ugh, why did you bring that up? Our first kiss was supposed to be magical."

Violet frowned. "It *was* magical. We're never alone together, and I wanted to know who you dated. It wasn't Kayla... Was it?"

Jess snorted and slapped his knee dramatically. "Kayla? Ha. She would never date me."

That wasn't the answer she wanted to hear, but at least one person was crossed off her list.

"Who was she, then?"

Jess raised an eyebrow. "Why did you ask if it was Kayla? Would it have mattered? And better yet, what will it change once you know who she is?"

Violet fidgeted with the zipper on her fleece hoodie and looked at the ground as she answered. "Because Kayla is pretty, and you've been friends with her for a long time. You have a lot in common. It would have made sense if you two dated."

"Well, we didn't. Feel better now?" Jess stood and held out his hand to her.

"Sure," Violet replied quietly. She grabbed her backpack from where she had set it on the ground and put her hand in Jess's.

They walked into the school together. Violet imagined everyone staring at them as they strolled through the hallway holding hands. Even though she had been dating Jess for weeks, this was the first time he had held her hand on the school grounds. Soon everyone would know that they were together. Maybe she could forget about trying to find out who Jess dated. She didn't know for sure that it was someone who went to their school. They could have moved away or transferred.

Either way, she needed to embrace the happiness in her life while she could. Being friends with Jess and Kayla, knowing they had dark intentions and secrets she hadn't uncovered, made every passing day feel like a ticking time bomb. She assumed they were waiting until they fully trusted her before they revealed the details of their plan. As the countdown went lower and lower until they started their plan, Violet didn't know what would happen when the time ran out.

The Quiet Girl

# Chapter 13:
# Before Jess

*September 6, 2019*

Even if they weren't as close as they used to be, Violet was thankful for her sister. At least she always had Emilia to turn to when things seemed bleak. Emilia already knew about her suspension, but Violet spilled everything—about Mallory and the tormenting she had endured for weeks, how she had finally snapped, and how she wanted to move back to Michigan. She never brought it up to their parents, since Abby had turned down the idea of moving in together without trying to make it work.

When Emilia got home from school on Friday, Violet's last day of suspension, she came into Violet's room, practically bouncing with glee.

"Why are you so happy?"

Emilia cheerfully hopped onto the burgundy suede chaise lounge in front of the window. "It's your last day of being suspended! You're free!"

"Yeah, but that also means I have to go back to school on Monday and face everyone. I would rather stay at home."

"Let's do something fun this weekend. Just me and you. We haven't hung out just the two of us in a while."

"Because you have friends and I don't," Violet reminded her in a snide tone.

Emilia sighed dramatically. "You can hang out with me and my friends."

"That's not what I meant."

"What? You don't want to hang out with middle schoolers?"

Violet gave her sister a side eye. "I mean, no. Not really."

"What do you want to do? Come on, let's hang out," Emilia persisted.

"Isn't that what we're doing right now?" Violet asked grumpily, throwing a pillow from her bed at Emilia.

Emilia karate chopped the pillow before it could hit her. "No, let's go somewhere. Have you gone downtown yet? There are some cool stores and restaurants there. I can ask Mom to drive us."

"She's still mad at me and I've barely talked to her this week. I doubt she'll want me going out and having fun," Violet retorted.

Emilia stood from the window seat and sauntered over to Violet, giving her the full effect of her pleading brown eyes. "She probably will if I ask her, though."

"Fine. If Mom agrees to drive us, then sure. We can go downtown."

***

*September 7, 2019*

It was a busy time at work for their mom—wasn't it always?—so their mom hadn't wanted to leave the house to spend the day being 'unproductive,' as she called it. Instead, Emilia asked their older brother, Glenn, promising to clean his room in return. He agreed.

Glenn dropped them off near a boutique clothing store and said to text him when they were ready to be picked up. He was going home to play video games all day. Typical.

Violet and Emilia spent the day wandering the downtown area. On one side of town, a surprising number of homeless people congregated in downtown Asheville. Buildings had been spray-painted with graffiti. There were tourist stores with '*I love Asheville*' T-shirts, coffee mugs, and magnets. The streets were narrow and parking was a nightmare, so they were thankful they both couldn't drive and that their brother had dropped them off. On the other side of town, there were trendy restaurants, an independent bookstore with a champagne bar, coffee shops, and unique stores selling anything from designer clothes to handcrafted furniture or expensive home décor.

When they noticed a bright red double-decker bus in the middle of a courtyard, Emilia squealed and stopped, wanting to check it out. Next to the bus were several tiny tables with concrete benches and red umbrellas to shield customers from the sun. The sign out front read 'Double D's Coffee & Desserts.'

"Want to see what it's like?" Emilia asked, her eyes wide with intrigue.

"Sure," Violet replied with a shrug.

She was mostly going along with whatever her sister wanted for the day. She appreciated that Emilia was trying to cheer her up, but she didn't think one day of shopping and exploring this eclectic city full of a strange mix of hippies, snooty North Carolina locals, and homeless people would make her feel better.

They entered the red double-decker bus and shut the door behind them. The air was warm and stuffy inside. The smell of freshly brewed coffee and baked goods permeated the air. To their right, a young woman with straight bangs stood behind a tiny counter with a cash register, a display of fresh cookies, and a chalkboard sign with the day's menu written in pink chalk.

"Hey, ya'll," the young woman said with a southern drawl. "Let me know if you have questions about the menu."

"Thanks," Emilia said, while Violet simply nodded.

Emilia ordered some sort of frappe that looked more like a dessert than coffee, while Violet went with her usual iced coffee. They each also purchased a cookie with their beverages.

"Let's see what the upstairs is like," Emilia said excitedly. She sipped her frappe and practically skipped up the stairs to the second floor of the bus. Violet trudged along behind her.

No one was upstairs. The top floor had several rows of red pleather bus seats with a small wooden table in front of each seat. Every few feet, yellow-lighted sconces lit up the walls. The large windows allowed customers to people-watch and witness the unusual things happening in Asheville.

Emilia sat on one of the front seats, looking out of the biggest window. Violet sat beside her and set her coffee and cookie on the table.

"Wanna hang out here for a bit?" Emilia asked.

"Sure."

Emilia playfully nudged her shoulder. "Hey, you're supposed to be having fun today, Vi. You're having fun, right?"

Violet attempted a weak smile, which made Emilia frown.

"*I'm trying*," Emilia said with sorrow clear in her voice.

Violet patted Emilia's shoulder and squeezed it. "I know. Thanks, Em. It's not your fault, though. One day won't change my life. It's just the way it is."

Violet blankly stared out of the large window and watched as a bird hopped through the courtyard by the parked bus, looking for crumbs people dropped as they passed through. She was thankful her sister cared about her happiness, but she couldn't pretend to be happy or that everything was fine because it wasn't. She didn't know how to fix it.

"The only thing that would make things better was if I could leave," Violet said.

"I don't want you to leave." Emilia stared at her in a rare moment of seriousness, her eyebrows scrunched together.

"Yeah, well, you're the only one." Violet fiddled with the straw in her coffee cup.

"That's not true. Mom and Dad love you. And Glenn does too, even if he can be a selfish brat most of the time." Emilia paused, sipped her coffee thoughtfully, then took a bite of her cookie. "What are you going to do?" She shifted beside Violet and turned to face her.

Violet sighed heavily. "I don't know."

"Is there a club or something you could join? Maybe that way you could meet some people and make friends."

"Maybe."

Emilia groaned obnoxiously. "If you want things to get better, you can't sit back and wallow in sadness. You don't want to be miserable forever, right? You need to change *something*."

"Yeah. I wonder if there's a book club I could join. That might be fun," Violet said, trying to be optimistic for her sister's sake.

"That's not exactly what I had in mind, but sure. Whatever works." Emilia sipped more of her frappe. "Nerd."

Violet laughed at her sister's childishness and finished her iced coffee. "Come on, let's shop a bit more before we text Glenn."

Emilia brightened up. She always enjoyed shopping more than Violet. "Yes! Sounds perf."

Violet and Emilia left the converted coffee shop and headed toward the part of the downtown area that they hadn't explored yet. As they crossed the street, Violet noticed a perky teenager with impossibly straight black hair and cold blue eyes. She made eye contact with the girl and a chill shuddered down her spine. It was Mallory.

# Chapter 14:
# After Jess

*September 30, 2019*

By the end of the school day, after Violet and Jess shared their first kiss, rumors flew around the school. Violet's life had finally seemed like it was looking up, but now it was crashing down around her again. Jess had kissed her outside of the school, where students walked by as they entered the building. Dozens of students had witnessed their kiss. Of course, it was blown out of proportion. An innocent first kiss witnessed by high schoolers turned into Violet and Jess half-naked, practically having sex in the courtyard. Everyone was calling her a slut, saying she seduced Jess and that she must have tricked him somehow because he had never stooped so low. He could date any of the girls in their grade. Violet had one guess about who spread the rumors.

When she and Jess met after their last classes ended, Violet stared at her locker, not quite believing what she saw. In what looked like fake blood, but upon closer inspection was red lipstick, someone had written SLUT in neat block letters on her locker.

Without saying a word, Jess wrapped her in a tight embrace and tucked her head underneath his chin. Violet didn't want to make a scene or start crying at school, so she did her best to remain calm and let Jess comfort her.

"I'm going to get some paper towels from the men's bathroom. I'll be right back, okay?" Jess promised.

"Okay," Violet said quietly, watching him walk away.

She stared at the locker, still in disbelief that Mallory would stoop so low. Why did she care about Violet dating Jess? Why was she doing everything she could to make sure her high school years were hell? The thought flitted through her mind. *What if Mallory was the one who dated Jess?* But she couldn't worry about that right now.

Violet hoped Jess would hurry back. She didn't want to stand alone in front of her disfigured locker for long. It was like the red 'A' in *The Scarlet Letter*. A mark on her spotless record. A symbol that she wasn't pure and innocent. A way to let everyone think her introversion was all a show. The ironic part was that she was still a virgin.

As Violet stood by her locker waiting for Jess to return, Savannah, one of Mallory's friends, approached her. Her long red hair swished around her waist, and her face was spattered with freckles.

Violet moved in a futile attempt to hide the vandalism, but of course Savannah had already seen it.

"Oh my goodness," Savannah said in a voice that oozed sweetness like honey. "I didn't think she would actually do it."

Violet stared at Savannah. "What do you mean? You know who did this?"

Savannah twirled her red hair around her finger in a carefree manner. "You don't strike me as a stupid person. I'm sure you can guess who did it. I thought she was only kidding. Otherwise, I would have tried harder to stop her." Savannah paused. "Before you clean your locker, if I were you, I would take pictures and document the situation, so you have proof."

"Why did she do it?"

Savannah continued twirling her hair around her finger, then let go. "Jess hasn't told you?" She tilted her head to the side and studied Violet.

Before Violet could form a coherent response or figure out what Savannah meant, Savannah had continued on down the hallway. A few minutes later, Jess came back with damp paper towels and hand soap. He handed Violet some of the paper towels, and they both started scrubbing her locker, doing their best to get rid of the evidence. At first, Jess insisted she should tell the principal what had happened, but Violet didn't care about reporting or documenting it, despite what Savannah said. All she cared about was erasing it and making sure her locker was blemish-free as if it had never happened. She didn't want to stand out, especially not for this. Besides, Principal Collins had made it perfectly clear that he wasn't a fan of Violet. She doubted he would do anything about this latest development. He would probably just blame Violet for what happened. Jess, however, took several pictures of her locker while the word was still visible, in case she changed her mind later.

After twenty minutes of intense scrubbing, Jess stood back and surveyed the locker. It still looked like a mess, although the SLUT part wasn't distinguishable anymore. Instead, the locker was smeared with red. Violet hoped the principal or janitor wouldn't think she did it. She didn't want to get in trouble for something she had no part in.

"I think that's as good as it will get for now. I can come to school early and help you clean the rest off tomorrow," Jess offered.

"It's fine. You don't have to do that." Violet picked up her backpack and walked toward the door at the end of the hall.

Jess quickly picked up his backpack and followed her, grabbing her hand and clenching it tightly as they walked through a crowd of students. Everyone gawked as they passed, whispering, snickering, and jeering, probably spreading more rumors.

"Are you coming to Big Beanz with me today still?" Jess asked once they were outside.

Violet hesitated. She didn't want to be in the public eye right now. If she stayed home, she could hope that things would die down and she could face people again. She shook her head. Besides, what had Savannah meant by 'Jess hasn't told you'?

"Not today, sorry."

Jess held both of her hands in his and stared deeply into her troubled eyes. "It's not your fault someone did that. I shouldn't have kissed you at school." He paused, biting his lip, and looked at her seductively. "I couldn't help it."

Violet smirked at him. "You better keep your hands to yourself for now. Until the rumors stop."

"Why do you care so much about what everyone thinks about you? Let it go. There will be a dozen more rumors by tomorrow, probably. Something else will happen that people will blow out of proportion and everyone will forget about our kiss."

"I know, but I don't like the attention. I don't want people to think I'm—"

"No one who knows you would ever think that. Besides, it was one little kiss."

"One kiss that could ruin everything."

"You're being dramatic," Jess teased her, pulling her closer.

"Jess, I'm not being dramatic! Do you even understand what I've been going through the past month and a half?" Violet broke away from him and folded her arms across her chest.

Jess grabbed her arms, gently trying to make her uncross them. "Hey, I know, trust me. I've had rumors spread about me, too."

"Yeah? Like what? Who would spread a rumor about you?"

Jess's eyes darkened. "You have no clue what I went through last year. Don't act like you know everything about me."

"You're right; I don't. Why don't you tell me what happened? Savanah implied something earlier..." Violet said, irritated that they seemed to argue in circles every time Jess alluded to his mysterious break-up and the worst year of his life. If Mallory was his ex, why didn't he just tell her and get it over with?

"Because I hate talking about it. And besides that, I don't want you to judge me."

Violet crinkled her nose. "Why would I judge you? Everyone in the school hates me. I'm definitely not going to judge you for whatever happened. It isn't your fault that your ex ended your relationship."

Jess leaned down and kissed Violet's forehead softly. "I promise I'll tell you, eventually. But it's not important. It has nothing to do with us. It's not like you've told me about all your ex-boyfriends."

"Well… There's not much to tell. I dated one guy earlier this year. We were friends for a while and dated for six months. He was my first boyfriend, my first kiss, and my first love."

"Whoa, that sounds like a lot to live up to." Jess leaned back against the exterior brick wall of the school. "Why did you break up with Mr. Perfect, then?"

Violet chuckled. "Why did you assume I ended things?" She shrugged. "I did, but that's beside the point."

"So…?" Jess prompted.

"When my parents told my siblings and I that we were moving, I broke up with him. I knew that long-distance would be too hard. We're too young to make something like that work." Violet smiled sadly as she thought about it. "I think I broke his heart. And it broke mine to do that to him," she said softly.

"Well, I officially feel inadequate. I better up my game to make sure your break-up was worth it."

Violet wrapped her arms around Jess's neck and pressed her lips against his. "It was worth it."

Jess took her hand as they headed to the parking lot. Violet tugged his hand to get his attention and make him stop walking.

"You were trying to change the subject. What did Savannah mean?" Violet chewed her lip and stared into Jess's green eyes, hoping it was nothing awful.

"It's not a big deal. I'll tell you later."

\*\*\*

*October 13, 2019*

Despite the chilly October air, Violet was laying in the hammock in her backyard with a worn paperback from the library. She had wrapped herself in her favorite fuzzy blanket, and she wore a heavy sweater with fleece leggings underneath her thick boots. The backyard was full of trees, although most were half-bare of leaves. The grass was browning, and the flowers she and her dad had planted when they moved in were wilting. When the cold closed in for the winter, the flowers would shrivel up and disappear.

Her phone buzzed in the pocket of her sweater, and she pulled it out to see the notification. It was a text from Jess.

**Jess:** Can I come over? I want to see you. :)

**Violet:** Like, now?

**Jess:** That's what I had in mind lol.

**Violet:** My parents are home though. They'll want to meet you if you come over.

**Jess:** :(

**Violet:** What?

**Jess:** Are you embarrassed by me?

**Violet:** NO! Of course not. Your parents are so much cooler than mine. If you come over here, they won't let us be alone.

**Jess:** Oh… so you want to be alone with me? I'm OK with this. Wanna come over later then? Do you think you can get a ride over here? ;)

**Violet:** LOL. I can ask my brother to drop me off. If I bribe him, he probably will.

**Jess:** Let me know!


Violet closed her book and carefully got out of the hammock. Once inside, she knocked on Glenn's bedroom door, not wanting to barge into her older brother's room. Who knew what he did in there all day?

"Yeah?" Glenn called.

She tentatively pushed the door open, wondering if this was her best option. "Hey, I have a favor to ask."

Glenn pulled off his headset and turned around in his swivel chair. He sat in front of his computer playing a video game, like usual. "What do you want?"

"Can you drive me somewhere in a bit? I can try to get a ride home. Please!" she begged her older brother, widening her eyes and pouting her lips.

Glenn looked at his computer screen and groaned obnoxiously, acting like it was the biggest favor in the world. "Fine, but I need to finish this mission, so you'll have to wait. My team is counting on me."

Violet resisted the urge to roll her eyes at how seriously he took his gaming hobby. He made it sound like it was life-or-death. But now wasn't the time to start an argument. "Sure, I'll go get ready then."

Violet shut Glenn's bedroom door and ran to her bedroom, taking the stairs two at a time. She needed to find something better to wear. She wasn't exactly wearing the most flattering outfit for hanging out with her boyfriend. Alone.

She pulled a black miniskirt out of her closet, put it over her fleece leggings, threw off her sweater, and chose a long-sleeve T-shirt. She looked at her reflection in the full-length mirror in her bedroom, went to the bathroom to brush her teeth, straightened her hair, and fixed her eyeliner that had smeared over the course of the day. As she contemplated if she should do something else to her hair, Glen yelled from downstairs.

"Violet! If you don't come down now, then I won't give you a ride!"

Violet quickly dabbed on some lip gloss and sprinted down the stairs, skipping every other step. "I'm coming!"

Glenn stood at the foot of the stairs, tapping his foot impatiently. "You owe me pizza."

"Deal."

Her brother was so simple. He didn't ask for much. All he needed to be happy was pizza and video games. Violet wished she could be more like him sometimes. For her, everything was so... complicated.

Violet input Jess's address into her phone's GPS and directed Glenn. On the way there, he glanced at her and asked, "So, is this a friend of yours?"

Violet's cheeks immediately flushed. She did *not* want to talk about boys with her brother. Besides, she hadn't even told her parents that she had a boyfriend. She had told them that Glenn was driving her to a friend's house to study for a test. It was the only way they would let her go out on a Sunday evening when she had school the next day.

"Yeah" was all she could make herself say.

"A *boy*?" Glenn asked with a knowing smirk as he focused on the road.

Violet turned to face him. "Don't you dare say anything to Mom and Dad."

Glenn waved her off. "I don't care that you're hanging out with a boy, but Violet... if he ever tries something you're not okay with and needs his ass kicked, let me know." His suddenly serious tone shocked her.

She hadn't expected that reaction. Sometimes she didn't think he cared about her at all. He certainly didn't act like it. "Thanks, Glenn, but Jess is a nice guy."

Glenn smiled grimly. "You never know. Guys can be assholes. Anyway, have fun." He pulled his car into Jess's driveway. "But not too much fun."

"Bye," Violet said hastily, exiting the car before he could try to give her a 'safe sex talk' or something else equally uncomfortable.

She texted Jess that she was at his house and stepped up to the front door, wondering if she should knock or wait for him to let her in. After debating what to do for several minutes, the front door opened.

"Hey. Are you going to come inside or what?" Jess asked with a grin.

"Hey," she said back as she entered the house.

Jess shut the door. "My parents are gone. Still at the coffee shop for a few more hours." His grin became even larger, and he held his hand out to her. "Come on, let's go to my room."

Violet took his hand and followed her boyfriend to his bedroom in the basement. She idly wondered if she should have come over to his house by herself for the first time when his parents weren't home, but it was too late now.

When they entered his bedroom, Jess sat down on his queen-sized bed. It was covered with a blue and black plaid comforter. The navy blue walls were plastered with classic rock band posters. There was a tiny bookshelf in the corner full of books, with some overflowing onto the floor. Across from the bed, there was a corner desk with a computer and double monitors. Why didn't that surprise her? It seemed like nearly every guy their age had an expensive computer.

"Join me?" Jess patted the spot on the bed next to him.

The only seating options were Jess's bed or the chair in front of his desk. Taking the computer chair would be weird, so she sat by him on the bed and nervously attempted to swallow down her anxiety. She hadn't thought this through, and she didn't know his expectations.

Jess brushed a few stray hairs from her face and rested his hand against her cheek, holding her face in his hands as he moved in to kiss her. Violet returned the kiss, and their kissing quickly became heated. Jess wrapped his arms around her waist and pulled her onto his lap, so she was straddling him. His hand hovered near the hem of her sweater, probably wondering if Violet would let him touch her breasts. He tugged her sweater up and touched her stomach, gently tracing lines across her waist and up her abdomen. As his fingers crept closer to her bra, Violet pushed him away, breathing heavily.

"Stop." Violet pulled her sweater back down and moved away from the bed.

Jess stood too, but remained a few feet away from her.

"Sorry! I thought you were fine with it," Jess said, scratching his head and looking at her as if he was confused.

Violet was embarrassed, but more importantly, she was unsure how far she wanted to go. They hadn't been dating long, and she didn't have a lot of experience. Jess had probably been with tons of girls.

"It's okay. I just... I'm not ready for that yet," Violet admitted as she tried to maintain eye contact.

"Oh. Are you...?" Jess trailed off.

Violet nodded slowly. "I'm a virgin." She paused, sizing him up. She thought she already knew the answer, but she wanted to be sure. "Are you?"

Jess shook his head. "No, but that's okay. We can take it slow. Sorry again if I was moving too fast. I just thought you were fine—"

"Who was she?"

"If you're wondering if it was the same girl I dated last year, then you're right. She took my virginity, then broke my heart," Jess said somberly.

"I'm sorry that happened to you."

Jess nodded. "Wanna get a snack?" He headed toward the bedroom door. He clearly didn't want to continue their conversation. "We can watch a movie in the theatre room."

Violet's jaw dropped. "Theatre room?"

"Yeah, I guess that's one perk of having wealthy parents when you're an only child. They can afford to do shit like that for me," Jess said with a smile.

She followed Jess back up the basement stairs and into the kitchen. He opened the pantry, which was stocked full of nearly every snack a teenager would enjoy: the large chip variety packs, beef jerky, cookies, candy, crackers, granola bars, and tons more.

"What do you want?" he asked.

"Chips are fine." She selected a small bag of regular Lay's potato chips.

"That's boring," Jess said with a laugh. He grabbed a bag of hot Cheetos, beef jerky, and a box of Chips Ahoy.

"For drinks, we have soda, water, juice, or tea?" He walked over to the fridge.

"Water is fine."

He handed her a water bottle and grabbed a Coke for himself. "Okay, now I'll show you the theatre room."

She followed Jess down the hallway, and he opened a door at the end of the hall. Above the door, a metal sign proclaimed, MOVIE THEATRE. He gestured for Violet to go first, so she entered and gazed around the room in awe. It wasn't a particularly large room, but for a home theatre, it was amazing. The walls were dark purple with framed movie posters hung every few feet. Blackout curtains covered the windows, and there were two rows with four seats each of authentic movie theatre style reclining seats, complete with cupholders. The seats in the second row were on a slightly raised platform, so the movie-watchers in front wouldn't block their view.

"Wow…" Violet said in amazement.

Jess grinned. "Yeah, my parents are both obsessed with movies."

There didn't appear to be a TV in the room, but when Jess pushed a button near the door, a projector slowly slid down from a slit in the ceiling, taking up almost the entire wall across from the entrance.

"This is ridiculous. But awesome," Violet said as she admired the room.

Jess plopped down in a seat in the back row and grabbed a remote. "What are you in the mood for? We have every streaming service you can think of, so pick whatever you want."

"Oh. Uh, what types of movies do you like to watch?" Violet sat in the recliner next to him and clumsily accepted the remote he handed to her.

"I like action movies, thrillers, horror movies… stuff like that."

"What about the new Marvel movie?"

Jess's eyes brightened. "Absolutely!"

They started watching the movie, ate their snacks—Jess demolished his much more quickly than Violet did—and they held hands throughout the movie. When it was almost over, the door to the room flew open, letting in a bright burst of light. Jess paused the movie, which froze on a scene where the antagonist was giving his 'this is my evil plan' speech.

"Hi, Violet," Jess's mom, Jasmine, said with a friendly smile.

Jess waved his arms around in front of himself obnoxiously. "Hello, I'm here too, Mom."

Jasmine came over to him and ruffled his hair affectionately. "Oh, I know, but I see you every day. What are you two watching?" She glanced at the projector screen.

"The new Marvel movie," Violet answered.

Jasmine nodded. "Christopher and I saw that one in theatres last month."

Jess raised his eyebrows. "What? You saw it without me?" He attempted to fix the hair that his mom had messed up. Before, it had been artfully messy. Now it was straight up disheveled.

Jasmine shrugged one shoulder. "We needed a date night. You were with your friends. Will you need a ride home, Violet?"

"Yes, please," Violet said.

"Let me know when you're ready to go home," Jasmine said as she left the room and shut the door.

Violet turned to look at Jess. "Your parents don't mind us being in here alone? With the door shut?" she asked incredulously. There's no way her parents would let her do that if she were at home with Jess.

"Yeah. They trust me."

"Apparently."

"Let's finish the movie. It's almost over."

Jess pressed play on the remote, and the action scene continued. They both remained quiet until the movie ended. The credits scrolled, and Jess fast-forwarded so they could watch the multiple after-credits scenes.

Violet wondered if Jess was mad at her for stopping him from going further earlier. She hoped not.

Jess turned off the projector screen and squeezed her hand reassuringly. "I'm not upset about earlier if that's what you're worried about." It was as if he read her mind.

Violet gave him a bewildered look.

"You were being quiet. Well, quieter than usual. So, I figured it was bothering you. We can take things slow. Let me know when you're ready and we can go from there. I won't pressure you into anything you don't want to do. Okay?"

Violet heaved a sigh of relief and felt like a weight had been lifted from her shoulders. "Thanks for understanding. Not every guy would have been so nice about it."

Jess frowned and squeezed her hand again. "Well, those guys are douchebags. I would never do that to you."

Violet smiled and kissed him softly. She felt so lucky to have the best boyfriend, someone who treated her right, respected her, made her laugh, and seemed to say all the right things. At last, things were looking up.

# Chapter 15: Before Jess

*September 7, 2019*

Violet grabbed Emilia's hand and pulled her into the closest store, which turned out to be a designer clothing store.

"I don't think she noticed me," she said, wheezing.

"What? Who?" Emilia asked, peering out of the store window.

The bell above the door jingled, and Mallory entered the store flanked by her entire gang: Jack, Savannah, Rose, and Izzy.

"Mallory," Violet hissed to her sister, pointing discreetly to the petite girl leading the group of teens.

Emilia's eyes widened in shock as she noticed Mallory and her friends. They were standing in front of the only door blocking their exit. "That's her? Oh, shit."

Violet's breathing quickened. She had never wished for an invisibility cloak more in her life. She prayed Mallory and her friends would ignore her, but she didn't have luck on her side.

"Oh, hello Violet," Mallory said with an evil smile. "I almost didn't notice you next to"—Mallory looked Emilia up and down and nodded approvingly—"Is that your sister? She looks like you, only pretty," she said with a cackle.

Emilia glared at Mallory. Despite being the younger sister, she put her arm protectively around Violet. "So, you're Mallory," she started, defiantly lifting her chin.

Mallory arched one of her perfectly shaped eyebrows. "You've heard about me?"

"Yes, and I don't like what I've heard. Now, if you'll excuse us, we were leaving," Emilia retorted haughtily.

Mallory snickered, and her friends followed suit. "Wow, Violet, your sister is braver than you are. You could learn a thing or two from her." She paused, appraising Emilia. "How old are you?"

Emilia stared directly at Mallory, not backing down. "Thirteen. I'll be in high school next year."

With that news, Mallory smiled sinisterly. "I'll keep my eye out for you then. You'll want to make sure you get in with the right crowd." She stepped away from the door to let Violet and Emilia pass.

Violet's face burned in embarrassment as she fled, shoving the store's door open and causing the bell to jingle obnoxiously. Emilia followed her.

"Let's get out of here. Now," Violet said in a panic. She began speed walking down the street in the direction they had come from earlier. "Can you text—"

"Already texted Glenn," Emilia said. She finished typing on her phone and slid it back into her leopard-print purse. "What happened to you in there, Vi? You froze."

Tears threatened to leak from her eyes. Violet stared at the ground, unable to make eye contact with her younger sister. Her sister, who Mallory liked after two seconds of talking to her. "I don't want to talk about it, okay?" She trudged to a bench further down the street and sat down.

Emilia listened to her sister's wishes, and they waited in silence for Glenn to pick them up. Violet couldn't stop herself from replaying the scene in the clothing store. Why couldn't she be more like her sister? Emilia was fierce and assertive. She stood up for herself and for Violet. Why couldn't Violet do that too? Violet dreaded going to school on Monday, certain that Mallory would have some fresh jokes about how weak and scared Violet had acted. Mallory would paint a picture of Violet as pathetic.

And she was.

The Quiet Girl

# Chapter 16:
# After Jess

*October 14, 2019*

On Monday morning, Violet woke up to multiple texts from Jess. Apparently, Kayla hadn't replied to his texts over the weekend and he was worried. With a start, Violet realized she hadn't heard from Kayla either. It was the first weekend since she became friends with Kayla and Jess that she hadn't seen Kayla or heard from her. It was strange, but she assumed everything was fine. Violet didn't know much about Kayla's home life and had never been over to her house. All she knew was that Kayla didn't like her mom's boyfriend, and he was apparently the person she wanted revenge on.

Jess wanted to go over to Kayla's house after school to make sure she was okay. Violet agreed, and Jasmine said she would pick them up from school and drive them there. They assumed Kayla could bring them both home later.

The school day passed normally. In the morning, Violet met Jess at her locker. The lipstick graffiti was long gone, but Violet still remembered how she felt when she found the SLUT mark on her locker.

Her morning classes were boring, and she barely paid attention, hiding a paperback inside her textbook to make it look like she was following along with her teachers' lectures.

During lunch, she met up with Jess and they ate at their usual table. Violet expected Kayla to join them.

"Have you seen her today?"

"No," Jess replied, his lips set in a bitter frown. "I'm really worried about her, Violet. She rarely misses school. Something must be wrong. Something with her mom's—" Jess stopped himself before he finished his sentence.

"With what?" Violet asked.

Jess sighed and ran his hands through his curly, dark hair. "I guess I might as well tell you. When we go to her house, you'll probably find out, anyway." He broke off part of his roll and chewed slowly, which wasn't typical for Jess. "Her mom has been dating this guy off and on for a while. He... he's not a good person. He's emotionally abusive, but he's also hit Kayla and her mom a few times."

"What?" Violet gasped. "Oh my God, I hope she's all right. She told me she didn't like her mom's boyfriend, but I had no idea it was that bad. Do you... Do you think something happened?"

Jess nodded and set down his half-eaten roll, leaving the rest of his food untouched. "I'm starting to worry that he took things too far. I keep calling Kayla, but her phone goes straight to voicemail, and she hasn't answered any of my texts."

Violet took Jess's hand and rubbed it reassuringly. It was clear how much he cared about Kayla's wellbeing. It was sweet. "Your mom's still planning on driving us to Kayla's later, right?"

"Yup."

"So, we just have to get through the rest of the school day, then we can make sure Kayla is fine."

Jess wrapped his hands around Violet's and squeezed tightly. "I can't eat anymore. My stomach is in knots thinking about what Kayla's going through right now."

Violet felt the same way, worried about her friend and wondering what she had endured. She repeated to herself what she had told Jess. *We just have to get through the rest of the school day.*

\*\*\*

After school ended, Jasmine drove them to a small red brick house and dropped them off in the driveway. It was much smaller than Jess's house and even smaller than Violet's too. The overgrown grass in the front yard needed to be mowed, and the house siding could use a good pressure wash.

"Are you sure you don't want me to stick around to make sure she's fine? Maybe you should have an adult with you," Jasmine said worriedly as Jess and Violet exited the car.

Jess shook his head. "No, we'll be fine. We both have our phones, and we'll call you if we need help."

"Promise you'll be careful?"

"Of course, Mom."

Jasmine waved and after another moment of hesitation, she finally drove away. Jess steeled himself and faced the house.

"Kayla's mom is really forgetful and always loses her keys, so she keeps a spare key in the planter by the back door," Jess explained as Violet followed him to the back of the house.

In the backyard, a small cement patio had a door in front of it, leading into the lower level of the house. As Jess had promised, a small, whimsical llama planter stood to the left of the door. Jess dug his hand into the dirt and fished around for a minute until his hand came out holding a silver key.

He smiled triumphantly. "Told you it would be there."

Violet rolled her eyes good-naturedly. "I never doubted you."

Jess unlocked the door and carefully entered the basement first. No cars were in the driveway, and the blinds were closed, so it was impossible to know if anyone was home. The house had a two-car garage, so Kayla's mom and boyfriend could have parked their cars inside the garage.

Violet tried to search the basement, pulling out her cell phone to use the flashlight. But Jess flicked the switch on the wall near the door and looked at Violet with a bemused expression on his face. Violet put her phone away.

"The basement isn't huge, and Kayla's bedroom is down here," Jess said. "I don't think anyone else would be down here, so we're probably safe."

"Hello?" a hoarse voice called from a pile of blankets on top of a full-size bed on the other side of the room. "Mom? Is that you?"

"Kayla, it's us. Jess and Violet," Jess said calmly, approaching the bed.

Violet followed closely behind him.

Kayla shielded her eyes with her hands, most likely squinting because of the sudden brightness of the lights. "What are you guys doing here?" Her voice was scratchy, and she sounded like she was sick. She kept her hands in front of her face like a shield. Her purple hair was matted and greasy, like she hadn't washed it in days.

"Kayla? Are you all right? We came here to check on you. I was worried when I didn't hear from you all weekend and you weren't at school today…" Jess trailed off.

"I'm fine," Kayla croaked in her strangely hoarse voice. She cleared her throat. "Thanks for coming by, but it wasn't necessary. I'm sick. With a cold. I'll be back at school in a few days."

Jess sat on the bed and peered at their friend. "Kayla, it's me. Your best friend. You can be honest. What's wrong?"

"I told you, Jess! I just have a fucking cold!" Kayla screamed, dropping her hands from her face in her anger and revealing a line of bruises across her face and throat.

Violet gasped in alarm and rushed over to Kayla. "Are you okay? I'm sorry we dropped by like this, but we were worried. Please tell us what's going on. We're your friends. We can help you."

Kayla slowly sat up in bed, grunting as if it took a great effort for such a simple task. Violet wondered how extensive her other injuries were, and if they looked as bad as her face. *It must be so painful.*

Kayla looked at Jess. "It was him. *Jimmy.*"

Jess sighed with recognition. "I figured. That's why I knew I needed to see you. How bad is it?"

"This is the worst it's ever been. My mom was trying to leave him on Friday, but he lost it. I went upstairs to get dinner because I hadn't eaten all day. and it was after 7 in the evening. I couldn't hear them fighting from down here, so I didn't know what was going on. If I had known, I wouldn't have gone upstairs…"

"What did he do to you?" Jess peered at her intently.

Kayla grimaced and held her hand against her rib cage as she leaned back onto the headboard of the bed. "When I walked into the kitchen, I saw him screaming at my mom, and he smacked her across the face. Hard. I decided I would rather go to bed hungry than be a part of their fight, so I turned back. I must have stepped on the creaky floorboard. You know the one."

Jess nodded.

"Jimmy started yelling at me and saying I was interfering with their adult conversation. That I was a nuisance, and it was all my fault they never had alone time. He said my mom would be better off without me. I know it was stupid, but I was so angry. I just wanted him to leave. So, I talked back to him and he started hitting me. And my mom… she…" Tears slipped from Kayla's eyes and fell onto her pale blue blanket, leaving water marks. "She just let it happen."

Jess gritted his teeth. Violet's stomach churned. She felt like she was going to be sick.

"When's the last time you ate?" Jess asked, with concern clear in his voice.

"I don't remember," Kayla said softly, laying back down on her bed.

"We'll get you something to eat and some painkillers," Violet offered.

"No, I don't know if he's here still. He might be upstairs. *You can't go up there*," Kayla warned them, suddenly frantic. "Jess, you know where my bathroom is down here. I think there's Tylenol or something in there?"

Jess went off to search for the painkillers, while Violet waited with Kayla. Violet dug around in her purse, pulling out a granola bar that she usually saved for occasions when she needed a random snack or on days when she didn't eat breakfast before leaving for school.

"Here." She handed it to Kayla.

Kayla smiled weakly. "Thanks." She unwrapped the granola bar and took a small bite, chewing slowly. She swallowed and winced. The bruises on her throat probably made eating painful.

Jess returned with a glass of water and a bottle of painkillers. "I found them." He passed them to Kayla and watched as she took a sip of water and downed two pills. "But, Kayla, this can't happen again. It's time."

Kayla nodded and sipped more of the water.

"Time for what?" Violet asked curiously, wondering what they were talking about.

"We're going to let you in on our secret, Violet. It's time for you to learn Kayla's deep, dark desire."

\*\*\*

Jess's phone buzzed with a text notification. Violet leaned over his shoulder to see who texted him. His mom.

Jess's eyes widened as he read the text, then he nodded resolutely as he texted his mom back. "Apparently, my mom didn't go home. She was worried about leaving us here alone, so she parked down the street and waited. Then she thought we had been inside the house for too long, so she wanted to make sure we were okay. She asked if she should call the police, but I told her we're fine." Jess turned to Kayla. "We'll help you pack a bag. You're coming with us."

"You can stay at my house," Violet blurted out, wanting to help and not thinking it through. Surely, her parents would understand after hearing about Kayla's situation.

Kayla looked back and forth between Jess and Violet unsurely, then said in the quietest voice Violet had heard her use, "Okay. Let me use the bathroom and try to cover up my face first. I don't want everyone to freak out when they see me."

Violet nodded in understanding. It was probably best if Jasmine and Violet's parents didn't know about the abuse. For now, at least. They would figure out a long-term solution later.

After Kayla emerged from the bathroom a few minutes later with her bruises covered with makeup and hidden as much as possible, she handed her toiletries to Violet, who obliged by packing them into a duffel bag she found in Kayla's closet. Kayla threw several jeans, hoodies, band T-shirts, underwear, and bras toward Violet. Jess blushed and looked away when he noticed Kayla's underwear and bras flying through the air. Kayla also stuffed her textbooks, notebooks, car keys, and cell phone charger into her backpack.

Jess approached Kayla when he saw her grab her car keys. "You can't drive like this. My mom will drive us to Violet's house."

"I need my car," Kayla insisted. "Otherwise, I'll have to come back here again. And neither of you has your license yet."

Jess looked unconvinced, but Violet knew Kayla was right. Kayla was the only one of the three of them who could legally drive.

"What if we go outside and reassure Jasmine that we're all right? Tell her Kayla will stay with me, and then she can leave?" Violet suggested.

Jess immediately shook his head. "That doesn't make sense. Then I'll need a ride home later."

"Right. Jess, you should go home with your mom now. I'll drive Violet and I to her house. We'll see you at school tomorrow," Kayla said resolutely.

"That makes the most sense," Jess said. "We'll work on the plan tomorrow after school, then?"

Kayla and Violet agreed. The trio left Kayla's house, locking the basement door behind them. Jasmine was waiting down the street, so they walked to her car and told her the bare minimum that she needed to know about the situation. She didn't seem happy that they wouldn't tell her everything, but she was relieved that Kayla was okay.

Violet sat in the passenger seat of Kayla's car while Kayla drove them to her house. Violet wasn't sure what to say, so they lapsed into silence for the drive, until Kayla pulled her car up in front of Violet's house.

Kayla faced Violet, taking her hands off the steering wheel as she put the car into park. "We need to decide how much to tell your parents. Do we tell them what we told Jasmine? That my mom and her boyfriend had a fight and I need somewhere to crash for a few nights until they cool off?"

Violet twisted her hair around her finger anxiously. "Yeah, I think so. I'm sure they'll be understanding."

And they were. Kayla stayed with Violet and they were all safe. For now.

The Quiet Girl

# Chapter 17:
# Before Jess

*September 9, 2019*

Rumors circulated around the school about Violet. She wasn't strong enough to stick up for herself, but her thirteen-year-old sister was a badass. Violet couldn't fight her own battles. She had moved to Asheville because she was a social pariah at her old school too. None of the rumors were true. In fact, Violet had a decent number of friends back home in Michigan. It took her a while to open up to people, but if she met someone she liked and had things in common with, she was easy to get along with. She attempted to ignore the rumors swirling around her as she walked through the school, but it was difficult. Plus, with how obsessed her classmates were with social media, it's not like the rumors were only being spread by word-of-mouth. Now everyone was posting things about her online too. Nowhere felt safe for Violet outside of her home.

Emilia had even seen the rumors online and told her to do something about it. Violet knew it was bad if her little sister, who didn't attend her school, had seen the lies about her online. Emilia was active on social media and had a large following, so maybe someone had shared the posts about Violet with her. By now, most people had probably made the connection that they were related.

Violet felt herself spiraling into darkness once again, wondering how she was going to find her way out of the mess she had become trapped in. After the incident when she slapped Mallory and had been suspended from school, she didn't feel safe going to talk to the principal. She hadn't talked to her parents much since everything had started. They were livid about the suspension, and Violet's mom frequently worked late nights and weekends, so she hadn't been home a lot since they arrived in Asheville. Her dad, however, barely knew what was going on with Violet and her siblings. He was forced to maintain the household, since Violet's mom always seemed to be gone, and lately he had been busy enough doing all the cooking, cleaning, grocery shopping, driving Violet and Emilia around—or forcing Glenn to chauffeur them—taking the kids to appointments, Emilia to cheerleading practice, and on and on.

Violet had run out of options and didn't know who else to turn to, if not her parents. Abby had barely spoken to her in weeks, since Violet had yelled at her and hung up on their video chat. Violet assumed Abby was busy with her new boyfriend, Scott, and that she didn't have time for Violet anymore. She texted Abby, not expecting a response, but she didn't want to give up on their friendship yet. She still hoped Abby could visit soon. Violet thought spending time with her oldest and closest friend would cheer her up. There was nothing more she could do. She only hoped that things would get better if she waited it out.

# Chapter 18:
# After Jess

*October 16, 2019*

When Violet asked her parents if Kayla could stay with them temporarily, at first, they had wanted to contact child protective services and report Jimmy. Violet's dad was wary about the situation, but he promised Kayla that he wouldn't let anything happen and that she would be safe while she stayed with them. Violet's house had a security alarm and outdoor cameras that her parents activated at night, so they would notice anything suspicious. Kayla didn't seem particularly worried about Jimmy coming there to find her, but Violet's dad insisted he would take care of it if Jimmy found out where Kayla was staying.

Violet adjusted to Kayla living with her. Even though they had known each other for a month now, they hadn't had the chance for a sleepover or to spend much time one-on-one together. She had learned more about Kayla in the past two nights than she had in the month before that.

The biggest adjustment was learning how to share the bathroom between Violet, Emilia, and Kayla. They had to make a schedule for their morning and nighttime bathroom routines to make sure they each had enough time to get ready. Also, Violet no longer needed a ride to and from school with Kayla living there. It was a welcome change to not have to wait for her sister to get ready for school and leave at the last possible minute every morning.

When Violet and Kayla arrived at school on Wednesday morning, Violet automatically knew it would be a shitty day when she approached her locker to find Mallory standing in front of it with Savannah beside her. Mallory's arms were crossed defiantly against her chest, and Savannah was brushing her bright red hair that fell to her butt. She stopped brushing when she noticed Violet and tapped Mallory on the shoulder, whispering to her. Violet was glad Kayla was still with her.

Violet couldn't open her locker to retrieve her textbooks, since Mallory and Savannah were blocking it, so she stood several feet away from them and waited. She didn't want to initiate the conversation and knew Mallory's ego would get the best of her and she would eventually reveal whatever she wanted.

However, Violet didn't consider that Kayla was with her this time. And Kayla wasn't one to stay silent.

"What do you want, Mallory?" Kayla asked, mimicking her stance with her arms crossed over her chest.

Mallory smirked and glanced at Violet. "Oh, nothing. Just wanted to congratulate you on your new *boyfriend.*"

Violet's face paled, and she tried not to let Mallory see that she was shaking. *Mallory knows about Jess? Why is she bringing him up?*

Kayla uncrossed her arms and clenched her hands into fists, looking at Mallory with her eyes narrowed, almost as if she was warning her. "Jess's relationship status is none of your business," she hissed.

Mallory laughed breezily. "It is, though. In case you don't remember, Kayla, I dated him first," she said gleefully, then whipped her head to the side to see Violet's reaction.

*What. The. Fuck.*

Violet couldn't form any words. The thought had crossed her mind before, but she had dismissed it because she couldn't picture Jess with someone like Mallory. After finding out that her worst fear was true, her brain felt like it had been blended into a pile of slop, like one of her mom's organic smoothies. No discernable thoughts or ideas. Just one big blob of incoherent questions.

"*You're* the one who broke up with *him*!" Kayla practically yelled. "And that was last year. He's moved on, and Violet treats him a hell of a lot better than you did."

Mallory tossed her glossy black hair over one shoulder and pouted her thin lips. "I may have been the one to end things, but I decided I want him back. We've been sleeping together for a few weeks now." Mallory smiled in a way reminiscent of Maleficent.

"What? You're lying!" Violet exclaimed, finally finding her voice in her shock. There was no way Jess would sleep with Mallory. He wouldn't cheat on her... would he?

Kayla shook her head violently. "He isn't sleeping with you. I bet he would rather fuck an old lady in a nursing home than your nasty self."

Violet laughed at Kayla's comment, and Mallory turned on her, her blue eyes shooting daggers.

"Why are you laughing? Your boyfriend is sleeping with me because you won't have sex with him. Maybe if you weren't such a prude, you could keep your man. I know how to keep him happy."

"Gross," Kayla said, crinkling her nose in disgust. "Come on, Violet, let's leave."

Violet silently followed Kayla down the hallway, but she could still hear remnants of Mallory's whispers as they walked away. She swore everyone in the hall was talking about her and Jess. Great. Now everyone knew she was a virgin, which was apparently the worst thing someone could be in high school, besides being a slut. As if that made any sense.

Kayla pulled her into an alcove toward the end of the hall and stood close to her, whispering so they wouldn't be overheard. "I know that was an awful way to find out that Jess used to date that bitch, but I swear that was the only part that was true. After what she did to him, he wouldn't go back to her. He's not sleeping with her. I know he really likes you."

"Why didn't he tell me?" Violet asked, crestfallen at the revelation and the wild rumors circulating around her.

"Because Jess knew Mallory had it out for you, even before you two were together. Something about you really pissed her off. He thought it would upset you if you knew they dated last year."

"Ugh, I feel so stupid. Why would Jess like me if he can get a girl who looks like Mallory?"

Kayla smiled kindly. "Violet, you're pretty, and Jess isn't so dumb that looks are all he cares about. You guys have something good; don't let Mallory ruin your relationship. Jess is my best friend. He would have told me if he was talking to Mallory again. She's trying to rile you up, to make you doubt things and break up with him, so she can try to sink her claws into him again. It's just a game for her. She doesn't care about him."

"I know you're probably right. But she's... she's the worst person I could imagine him being with. I literally would have rather found out he dated anyone else!"

"Tell me about it. He was a nightmare when he was dating her. He did everything for her, and she was a complete bitch."

"Why did they break up?" Violet asked, then instantly wondered if she wanted the answer.

"She cheated on Jess with Tanner. Jess saw naked photos on her phone and realized she was cheating. Apparently, sex with Jess wasn't enough for her, which is why it wouldn't make sense for them to get back together," Kayla said with a shrug.

Jess walked up to them and joined them in the alcove, panting. "There you are! I've been looking all over the school for you," he said as he wrapped his arms around Violet.

Violet pushed him away, not in the mood for a hug from him after what she had just learned. "We need to talk."

Kayla's gaze bounced nervously back and forth between Violet and Jess, and she stepped out of the alcove. "I'll leave you two alone. See you at lunch!" she called as she left.

Violet stared coldly at Jess. Even if Mallory had lied about sleeping with Jess recently, she wanted to hear the truth from him. "Mallory told me some very interesting news."

Jess looked at her expectantly, oblivious to what had happened. "Yeah?"

"I know she's the one you dated, and she's the one who took your virginity. She confronted me earlier, and she was gloating about it. She must have found out we were dating." Violet paused, reflecting on something Mallory had said that she hadn't thought much about until now. She had been too preoccupied with the horror of finding out that Jess had dated her bully. "Wait a second. She knew I was a virgin and threw it in my face that she had sex with you, and I wouldn't. How did she know that?"

Jess's face reddened considerably. He rubbed the back of his neck, where his dark brown curls were becoming unruly. He needed a haircut. "I-I'm not sure," he stuttered. "Can we talk about this later?"

"No, we're talking about this now." Violet stared at him boldly, refusing to back down. Not this time.

# Chapter 19: Before Jess

*September 10, 2019*

After Violet reached out to Abby and apologized for how she had acted, their friendship had been shaky. Violet wanted to see her best friend and to feel like her life was normal again, so she begged Abby to visit. Three days later, Abby finally responded to Violet's request. She booked a plane ticket for a long weekend over Thanksgiving break. But it was only September, so Thanksgiving was still over two months away. Violet wished the time would pass more quickly. She couldn't wait to see Abby and knew that was what she needed to bolster her happiness. Seeing Abby would make things better.

Violet had gotten into the habit of hanging out with Emilia and her friends on most weekends. At first, when Emilia offered, she declined, saying she was too busy with homework. But as weekend after weekend passed, and she spent her free time holed up in her bedroom obsessing over her schoolwork and the rampant rumors, she conceded at last. And she was glad she did.

It shocked Violet how much fun she had hanging out with middle schoolers. They were only two years younger than her, and it really wasn't that much of an age difference. They still had things in common, like the movies they watched and music they listened to, so Violet didn't feel out of place with them, unlike when she was around some of her peers at the high school who partied like college students.

Violet's life was bearable for the moment. It's not like she was best friends with any of Emilia's friends, but she was thankful they had let her into their little circle. All of them were sympathetic about what was going on with her and were understanding about how she felt. It was a pleasant change to have people to talk to who seemed to care about her. She was lucky to have Emilia as her sister, always looking out for her and willing to help however she could. At least for the moment, Violet was fine.

# Chapter 20:
# After Jess

*October 16, 2019*

The ball rang, interrupting their conversation.

"Look, can we talk about this at lunch or something?" Jess asked, scratching the back of his neck and looking around the hall at the students milling around.

It seemed like everyone stared at them and whispered. News spread fast in high school, especially when Mallory was involved.

Violet grabbed Jess's arm when he turned, as if he was about to leave in the middle of the conversation. "No! What are you hiding from me?"

Jess sighed loudly and stepped back into the alcove, sitting on the window bench and patting the seat next to him. Violet sat beside him, attempting to keep as much distance between them as possible. The halls emptied as students scurried to class. She had a perfect attendance record, but she didn't care about ruining it at that moment.

"You're right. I dated Mallory last year. When she paid attention to me over the summer before high school started, I was excited. Who wouldn't be?" He backtracked when he saw the look on Violet's face. "I got caught up in it all—her parents' crazy wealth, the popularity, the attention, having so many friends, the social life, and of course how gorgeous she is. I know it's stupid, but I really thought I was falling in love with her. We spent almost every day together that summer. By the time school started for freshman year, she started acting differently. She became more distant as time passed. When her parents were out of town, she invited me over to her house to stay the night. She seduced me and convinced me to have sex with her. I was unsure about making such a big decision, but she talked me into it. Afterward, I felt awful—like she used me for sex. She wasn't a virgin and had dated tons of guys—I knew that when we got together—but I thought maybe things would be different with us. I thought she cared about me," he said, sounding choked up, looking down at his designer shoes. He looked back up at Violet after a moment. "After that night, we drifted apart and spent less time together. I was frantic. I didn't want to lose her, so I became obsessive, trying to keep tabs on her, constantly asking who she was texting and what she was up to on the weekends. Then, when we were at a party a few weeks later, she disappeared and left her phone with me. Somehow, I got the idea into my head that I needed to check her phone. I suspected she was cheating, but I needed proof. When I searched her phone, I found sexy pictures she had taken and sent to Tanner, one of my close friends at the time. I went looking for her and finally found her in one of the bedrooms, making out with Tanner, nearly naked. I remember punching him and all Mallory did was scream at me to leave so she could 'have sex with a real man.'" Jess shook his head sadly. "She messed me up, and I'm sorry for dragging you into this mess. I think it's partially my fault that she targeted you. She wants me to be miserable and is trying to hurt me in any way she can. I stood up to her that day when she was bullying you in the cafeteria, and that really pissed her off."

"I'm sorry about what happened, Jess. That's terrible the way she treated you. Plus, cheating on you with one of your friends? That's harsh. But—how did she know I was a virgin? And why did she say you two were together again? Have you been talking to her?" Violet's words tumbled out as she tried to sort through her confused, painful thoughts.

"I screwed up, Violet. After you left my house this weekend, I texted her in a moment of weakness. She immediately called me, and I fell back into old habits and spilled my guts to her. I don't know how she does it, but she convinced me to tell her what was going on with you. I swear nothing happened. All we did was talk on the phone. I'm sorry I told her about you. I didn't think she was so cruel that she would tell everyone, but I should have known better. I shouldn't have trusted her."

Violet straightened her posture and stood from the bench, making herself as tall as possible, and picked up her backpack. "Nice chatting with you, but I'm already late for class."

She stepped out of the alcove and Jess quickly grabbed her arm, trying to stop her from leaving.

"Let go of me!" she shouted, almost wanting someone to hear and think Jess was hurting her so he would get in trouble.

Jess dropped his hand from her arm. "Please don't leave." His eyes shined with tears. "I can't handle this right now. *I need you*," he said, his voice fierce with emotion.

Violet shook her head. "No, you don't. I think we need to take some time apart. I need to—think about things—about us." She stared into Jess's eyes, his green eyes she had once found so beautiful and warm. "I don't think you're good for me."

Violet left the alcove and walked to class, leaving Jess alone. She had finally stood up for herself. So why did she feel so terrible?

\*\*\*

During her lunch period, Violet impatiently waited in line to buy food, then exited the cafeteria. It was chilly outside in the courtyard, but not so cold that it was unbearable. She sat on a bench, alternating between turning the pages of her newest book and munching on fries, when she realized someone was standing next to the bench. She half-expected it to be Jess trying to apologize or Mallory with a fresh way to torment her. When she tore her eyes away from her book, she noticed with relief that it was neither of them. It was Kayla.

"Can I join you?" Kayla asked.

"Sure."

Before Kayla could say anything about Jess, Violet blurted out, "I don't want to talk about Jess. I'm sure he told you what happened this morning. We're... taking a break."

"He talked to me and he's so upset, Violet. He knows he screwed up by talking to Mallory." Kayla lowered her voice and scooted closer to Violet on the bench. "If it makes you feel any better, I'm still a virgin too," she confided with a small smile.

Violet laughed and closed her book, tucking it into her backpack. "Good to know I'm not the only prude at this school."

Kayla responded by hitting her playfully with her lunch tray. "Nope, there's a bunch of us here. You just have to search for them." Kayla paused and stared down at her lunch tray for a few seconds. "Are you okay, though—"

Violet finished the last of her fries. "I'm serious. I don't want to talk about him."

The wind blew across the courtyard, ruffling the bare tree branches. The sky seemed foreboding as it darkened and Violet shivered, zipping up her hoodie all the way to her chin.

"Okay, fine. We'll talk about something else. We're two smart teenage girls; there are a dozen other things we could talk about besides a dumbass guy," Kayla said.

"Did you only come out here to convince me to get back together with him? Because if you did, you should probably leave."

"No. I've been friends with Jess a long time, but I care about you too. Although it might screw with our fucked up little trio, I want to be friends with both of you, even if you don't want to date him anymore."

"Well, that's a relief. I wasn't sure if you only hung out with me because of Jess."

"At first, maybe. He was completely smitten with you. It was annoying, but once I got to know you, I understood why he felt that way about you. You're pretty great."

"You're not too bad sometimes either," Violet replied cheekily.

Kayla responded with an eye roll, dissolving any cheesiness that had happened. "I'm also still living with you, so I hope this doesn't make things awkward," she added.

Violet sighed, thinking about everything Kayla had gone through recently. Kayla living at her house was only a temporary solution. She didn't know how she could help Kayla long-term. Her parents wouldn't let her stay there forever. And Violet assumed Kayla's mom would want her to come home at some point. Apparently, Jimmy was still in the picture and they hadn't resolved the situation. Not that Violet even knew how to fix such a terrible thing.

"Right. Speaking of which, are you going to tell me about your deep, dark desire? Or do I have to guess?"

Kayla nodded slowly. "I suppose I should tell you. But once you know, you're in too deep to get out. It will be too late to back out of this. You have to help me." She cleared her throat and leaned back against the bench, looking at Violet seriously. "I want to kill Jimmy."

# Chapter 21
# Before Jess

*September 11, 2019*

Violet didn't see how her life could get any worse. But she had endured a lot of days like that recently. Every time she thought *surely, things can't get worse*, that seemed to be around the time when something else happened.

She sat in her Spanish class, wondering for the hundredth time why she had ended up in the same class as Mallory. It felt like a cruel twist of fate to be forced to suffer through a class, with her tormentor sitting right behind her. Mallory seemed to find every opportunity she could to bother Violet or attempt to get her in trouble. She would constantly poke her in the back during class with a pen, trying to elicit a reaction from Violet. She and the other students teased her for bringing a book with her everywhere. They made fun of her clothes, her hair, how awkward and quiet she was—basically anything that made Violet stand out was fair game.

One day, Mallory's friend Rose even made farting noises periodically throughout the class period and blamed Violet, to which Señora Iliza scolded Violet and asked her to stay after class. To some students, it may have seemed like harmless teasing, but to endure such things daily, and ceaselessly, would wear on anyone after so long. To make matters worse, Violet also couldn't do anything to stop it after the incident that led to her suspension. She knew Principal Collins would only end up taking Mallory's side again.

Now that everyone in the school also thought she was a wimp whose thirteen-year-old sister had to fight her battles for her, she was even less likely to say anything. Because deep down, Violet knew it was true. She couldn't stick up for herself because she was scared of the consequences. If Violet called out Mallory and told her to stop, she didn't know what would happen. She could only imagine how Mallory would retaliate. So, wasn't it better to accept that this was her life now? Complacency was usually best, no matter how terrible the situation was.

Violet sank into a deep depression, unlike anything she had known. She barely ate, she stayed locked in her room most of the time and barely left the house except to go to school—all she wanted to do was lie in her bed and sleep or read. The only miniscule amount of joy she found was in the books she read, which offered a welcome escape from her miserable existence. She preferred the fantastical and supernatural, anything that was as different from her own world as possible.

As she sank deeper, Violet's grades actually went up. She had zero social life and nothing better to do than focus on her homework and studying, so her studiousness was reflected in her straight As. Her stellar grades impressed her parents, and they promised to buy her a used car for her sixteenth birthday if she kept it up. That was motivation enough to keep working hard. Her sixteenth birthday wasn't until the end of October, the twenty-eighth, just before Halloween, so she would still have to wait a little over a month for the car, but it was something to look forward to.

***

After school, Violet spent her night how she spent most nights: curled up in bed with a book, a pile of highlighted notebooks and textbooks, and a movie she had watched a hundred times playing on the flat-screen TV in her bedroom. Often, she wished things had turned out differently, but she had learned that she needed to accept the way her life was and try to make the best of it. Maybe she could convince her parents to let her transfer to remote learning. It was becoming more popular, and after some research, she discovered that her high school offered a remote learning program. The point was— she had options, and she wasn't using them because of her fear of approaching her parents. But she knew she had to if she wanted to feel safe and happy ever again.

The only problem was that both of her parents never seemed to be around at the same time. They co-parented and split up their time and responsibilities with their kids like a divorced couple. They tried to make their relationship as 50/50 as possible. Violet always thought their relationship was weird and wondered why they stayed married. They were like strangers who slept in the same bed.

When her mom finally walked into the house after work, it was nearly 7 p.m. Violet's dad, William, had cooked dinner for the kids like usual and they ate together without Violet's mom. Jocelyn worked long hours during the week, and she usually slept in on the weekends. This minimized the time she spent with her family, and Violet couldn't remember the last time they had all done something together. Definitely not since they had moved to Asheville.

Violet greeted her mom. "Hey."

Jocelyn set down her bag, mumbled an incoherent reply, and immediately shot for the coffeemaker, turning it on, scooping coffee into the filter, and refilling the water reservoir. William shot her a look.

Jocelyn cleared her throat and stared at Violet with bleary eyes. "How's school, Violet?" She rummaged through the fridge for leftovers.

Violet paused thoughtfully. This was her chance. Her siblings had both gone into their bedrooms, so she had a rare opportunity to be alone with her parents. "I need to talk to you. To both of you."

William turned from his spot in front of the kitchen sink where he was washing dishes and shut off the sink faucet, drying his hands on a towel. "About what? Is everything okay, honey?" An expression of concern washed over his face.

Violet sighed as she sat on a kitchen chair at the circular wooden table in the center of the kitchen. "No, it's not."

"Should you really be drinking coffee this late?" William asked Jocelyn pointedly.

Her glare made him halt his protest.

William joined Violet at the table and beckoned to Jocelyn to sit down too. The coffee maker emitted a series of beeps and the water began heating. The smell of freshly brewed coffee filled the kitchen. Her mom waited until the coffee was ready, grabbed a mug, and filled it to the brim before she sat at the table with her husband and daughter.

"Okay, what is this about?" Jocelyn asked with trepidation. "Are you in trouble? You didn't get suspended again, did you?" Jocelyn narrowed her eyes and clenched her coffee mug in her fist.

Violet held back from getting upset. She needed her parents to be on her side, so now wasn't the time to argue the fact that the suspension hadn't been her fault. All she needed from her parents was for them to agree that she could take her classes online. It would solve most of her issues.

"Because of everything that's been going on at school—the bullying, the rumors, and I don't have any friends—"

Jocelyn opened her mouth as if she was going to protest, but William shushed her and motioned for Violet to keep talking.

Violet continued, "I would like your permission to transfer to remote learning. My school has an entire curriculum online. I would still have to go to the school for tests, but other than that, I can do all my work from home." She breathed heavily, as if she had just finished a strenuous hike. And in a way, she had. Talking to her parents together sometimes felt like climbing a mountain to get their attention.

William folded his hands on the table in front of him. "That sounds like a reasonable request. I know things haven't gone how you expected since we moved and—"

Jocelyn vehemently disagreed, waving her coffee mug around, the coffee sloshing onto the scuffed wooden table and the ceramic floor. "No, I don't think that's a good idea at all. Kids need to go to school in person. It's good for you to socialize, to be around other teenagers. Not everyone is going to like you. It's better that you learn that now while you're young and figure out how to cope with it."

William moved to the counter to grab a roll of paper towels and a mop to clean up the spilled coffee. As he wiped up the mess, he spoke. "This isn't a case of Violet not being liked. She's being bullied by that girl—"

"Mallory," Violet reminded him, as he looked at her for confirmation.

"Right. Well, I don't see why switching to remote learning would be an issue. In my opinion, it solves the issues Violet's been having at school and she'll be safe at home."

Violet felt relieved that things would work out until her mom jumped in.

Jocelyn set down her now half-empty cup of coffee on the table. "It's not such a straightforward decision as that—"

"Why on Earth not, Jocelyn?"

"Because, *William*, she's a child, and she can't make these decisions on her own. I know what's best for her," Jocelyn retorted.

"Do you, though? You're barely around enough to know what's going on with our kids, let alone what's best for them," William shot back.

Violet pushed her chair away from the table and stood. "I think I'm going to go back to my room," she mumbled, but neither of her parents paid attention to her as they continued their heated argument.

Violet retreated to her bedroom, her one safe place, and closed the door. *Well, that went well.*

# Chapter 22:
# After Jess

*October 24, 2019*

Violet and Kayla searched through the racks for Halloween costumes. They were at one of those pop-up stores that temporarily took up space in the mall for a few months every fall, then disappeared again after Halloween had passed. Halloween was only a week away, which also meant Violet turned sixteen in the upcoming week. October twenty-eighth. She always thought she would be more excited when she could finally drive, especially since her parents had surprised her by promising to buy her a car for her birthday, but with everything going on, she didn't care about the milestone birthday or the car. Besides, Kayla could drive already, so she didn't need to worry about getting places anymore.

Violet wondered if it was cheesy if they picked out matching costumes. Before last week, she would have assumed that she and Jess would coordinate their costumes, but now? Definitely not. She strolled through the store, gazing at slutty nurse outfits, a zombie costume, a variety of wigs, an Alice in Wonderland dress, superhero outfits, Disney princesses, and a pirate costume that looked like a rip-off of Jack Sparrow's outfit in *Pirates of the Caribbean.*

Kayla nearly scared the shit out of her by tapping on her shoulder, forcing her to spin around and face her. She wore a grotesque-looking Pennywise mask and said, "We all float down here," as Violet shrank away. She was terrified of clowns.

"Sorry." Kayla laughed, pulling off the mask and discarding it on a random rack of costume accessories. "Any ideas?"

Violet shrugged and kept walking through the store, following behind Kayla. She decided to be bold and chose a Catwoman costume. She had always admired Selina Kyle. Kayla nodded approvingly at her choice, then showed Violet her selected costume: a female Jack Sparrow. She was all for it.

***

*October 26, 2019*

Jess texted her, saying he had a surprise for her birthday. He invited her over to his house on Saturday night. He told her to wear a Halloween costume and said they would pass out candy to trick-or-treaters. The idea was sweet, and she always enjoyed seeing the young kids dressed up in their adorable costumes.

She was willing to give him a chance to apologize, but Violet was hesitant to accept his apology, assuming that he would try to make it up to her. She still wasn't sure she wanted to get back together with him. Maybe she would forgive him, but she didn't know if she wanted to date someone who spilled details about her extremely personal choices to the girl who hated her. That didn't bode well for their future. Not to mention the fact that he had apparently dated the girl who had been bullying her since her first day at school. What did that say about Jess since he had been okay with dating someone so cruel?

When she arrived at his house after her dad dropped her off, she walked up to the imposing front door, suddenly filled with anxiety. She hadn't felt nervous before, but now she wondered why she had to wear her costume. She felt silly all dressed up and regretted her costume choice, thinking she overdid it. But then the front door swung open, revealing Jess dressed in a black spandex suit nearly identical to hers, complete with a long black cape and a black mask covering most of his face.

A smile formed on her face and she shook out her glossy, straightened hair. "Nice to see you, Bruce."

Jess grinned and leaned in for a hug. "And you, Selina," he said in a gravelly tone much deeper than his usual voice.

"How did you know?" Violet asked curiously, as Jess brandished his cape and ushered her into his house.

"Kayla texted me."

"Oh."

"Disappointed?"

"No. Confused," Violet responded as she entered the foyer and stared in surprise at the entryway to the house.

Jess had fully decorated the house for Halloween. Fake spiderwebs hung on the banisters of the staircase, the chandelier, and the light fixtures. Metallic streamers seemed to float from the ceiling. As they walked into the kitchen, Violet saw bowls of punch, what looked like enough trays of food to feed the entire high school, and various black and orange Halloween-themed desserts.

Violet instantly wanted to turn around and leave when she realized why Jess really invited her over. "You tricked me."

"No, no. I'm sorry. I wanted to do something nice for your birthday. It's a surprise party," he said, smiling sheepishly and gesturing around the room.

"My birthday isn't until next week" was all she could say. Despite her irritation with him for tricking her into attending a party with people who didn't like her, the fact that he had tried to do something nice for her was… surprising? It was clear he was trying to make it up to her. But she wasn't sure if it was enough. She still didn't know if she could trust him. And why had he chosen a surprise party? Did he even know her at all?

"Who did you invite?" she asked with a start. "The entire school hates me. Who would want to come to a party celebrating my birthday?"

"You'd be surprised," Jess said jokingly. "I told everyone I was having a Halloween party to celebrate your Sweet Sixteen. Most people were excited to have an excuse to party. They'll dance, drink too much punch, people will sleep together who shouldn't, and they'll all leave by midnight."

Violet nervously adjusted her spandex suit. Jess noticed and commented, "You look hot."

Violet blushed as she stopped messing with her costume. "Thanks."

"What? I don't get a compliment? I worked really hard on this costume," Jess teased.

Violet playfully poked him in his chest. "You know you look good. You don't need anyone to inflate your ego more."

"Oh, fine. Want some punch?"

Violet followed Jess into the kitchen and over to the punch bowl. Her nose crinkled as the aroma of the punch rose to her nostrils. "Um. What's in it?"

"Vodka, Hawaiian Punch, pineapple juice, orange juice, ginger ale..." he listed the ingredients. He shrugged as he poured a cup for himself. "I might have doubled the vodka in the recipe, though," he said with a wicked grin.

Violet grabbed a cup and poured some punch into it. She figured half of a cup would be fine. Maybe she would be less anxious if she were drunk. She and Abby used to sneak wine coolers from her mom's stash, so she had drank before, but never anything as strong as this punch. She willed herself not to gag when she took a sip, but the sweetness of the drink surprised her.

"It tastes like juice."

Jess served himself a cup of punch and took a few large gulps. "Yup. Danger juice."

Violet rolled her eyes at the name. "You're ridiculous. So, when is everyone else showing up?" He had told her to be there at 6 p.m.

"I told them 7, which means most people will be here closer to 8."

"What are we going to do until then?" She took another sip of the punch. *Screw it.* She threw back her head and downed the rest of her cup.

"Impressive," Jess said, raising an eyebrow. He finished his punch and served them each another drink. "Let's go into my room."

Violet protested, "No, I don't think so."

Jess's eyes softened, and he smiled at her in a kind manner. "I swear I won't try anything." He took a sip of his punch and gave her his best smolder. "Unless you want me to, of course."

She hit him on the shoulder and followed him to his bedroom, sipping her punch as she walked. By the time she sat on his bed, she realized she had nearly finished the second cup. The drink went down so smoothly; it didn't taste like alcohol at all. Jess was right in calling it "danger juice." She needed to be careful.

Jess sat on the bed next to her. "Whoa, maybe you should slow down?" he said as more of a question than a command when he realized her cup was almost empty. "I don't want you to think I'm trying to take advantage of you. *And* I don't want you to puke on my bed."

"I'm fine," Violet replied, enunciating her words and speaking slowly. She felt lightheaded, though. She probably needed to eat something before she drank any more. "What did you want to talk to me about?"

"I wanted to apologize again… about… well, everything. I acted like an ass. I am an ass. You didn't deserve that, and I'm sorry I texted Mallory. It was stupid of me to tell her what happened. I don't know why I did. Clearly, I wasn't thinking, and I'm worried that I ruined things with you." He looked down at her, his green eyes full of despair. Despair that seemed real.

"I accept your apology."

"Oh, thank God. I was worried you wouldn't want to get back together."

"I don't." Jess's face fell. "At least, not yet. Can we see how tonight goes?" Violet suggested.

Jess nodded. "That's fair. I can't expect you to want to be with me if you can't trust me. Tonight will be fun, I promise."

"I hope so."

***

Around 9 p.m., the party was in full swing. Like the inside of the house, Jess had also decorated the backyard with Halloween decorations. When Violet saw the extent of the décor, she assumed Kayla must have helped him. People mingled outside, in the kitchen, the living room, and the movie theatre room, where horror movies were playing. Kayla had picked out the movies, of course; her love of horror was legendary. People were drinking punch, dancing, and devouring the snacks. Jess had warned everyone to keep out of the bedrooms. His parents were out of town for the weekend for some type of business convention and they didn't care about him having a party, but they would be pissed if anyone went into the bedrooms, especially the master bedroom.

Violet tried not to cling to Jess, but she barely knew half the people at the party and wasn't sure why so many people showed up. She supposed they all wanted to drink, dance, and celebrate Halloween and didn't care that it was her birthday party. It was fine with her. She was having as much fun as possible while being surrounded by at least fifty teenagers. If she hadn't been drunk, she probably would have been a lot more nervous. But the punch dulled her anxiety and softened the edges of everything in her fucked-up life.

When she grabbed a paper plate and filled it with snacks from the kitchen, she nearly dropped her heavily laden plate when she saw who had entered the house. Her black hair was tied back in a loose ponytail and she had a sleek, black Catwoman suit stretched over her perfect body. She even had a belt around her waist full of tech gadgets. Violet looked down at her own costume, feeling inferior when she saw how much better Mallory looked in hers.

As she tried to stop comparing herself to her arch-nemesis, she wondered, *why is she here? And better yet, why did she have the same costume idea I did?*

Violet scurried away with her food, but Mallory spotted her before she was in the clear. Mallory poured herself a cup of punch.

"Violet! Where are you going?" Mallory trilled in a singsong voice as she stalked toward her. She paused in front of Violet, with her hip cocked to the side, one hand on her hip, and the other holding her punch.

"I—uh—" Violet stuttered brilliantly. "I like your costume."

Mallory smirked and gestured to her body. "Right? I fill it out in all the right places," she said cockily.

Rose piped up, "I saw you buying it at the costume store, so I told Mallory. I knew it would look better on her."

Violet hesitated, unsure how to respond to Mallory's inflated ego and Rose's spying. She turned to leave the kitchen; her plate of food forgotten. Violet had barely taken three steps into the hall toward the living room when a cold liquid sloshed down her back and she heard a cackle from behind her.

A female voice screeched, *"Mallory!"*

Violet touched the back of her costume and her fingers came away smelling like rum and juice. She whipped around, facing Mallory. "Did you just dump your drink on me?"

Mallory smirked and all her friends giggled, except Savannah, who had a horror-stricken look on her face.

Mallory slightly shrugged one shoulder. "I tripped. It was an accident."

Just then, Jess came into the room and rushed to Violet's side, as if he had sensed trouble brewing. "What are you doing here, Mallory?" he asked in a neutral tone, not wanting to start anything.

Violet grabbed his arm, attempting to tell him about the spilled punch, but Mallory cut in.

Mallory stepped closer to Jess and poked his chest with one of her manicured fingers, which were painted the color of blood. "Oh, Jess... you didn't think I would miss out on one of your parties, did you? Most of the cool kids are here. I assume my invitation was lost in the mail?" she suggested, her eyes glinting dangerously.

Jess shook his head. "Can you please leave without making a scene? The party is to celebrate Violet's birthday."

Mallory rolled her eyes and downed the entire cup of punch she was holding, then crushed the paper cup in her hand, letting it fall to the floor. "The least you can do is dance with me for one song," she pleaded, as she stuck out her bottom lip in a sexy manner that Violet assumed Jess would agree to.

But he surprised her. "I don't think that's a good idea," Jess stated, as he closed the distance between himself and Violet and put his arm around her protectively. "This night is all about Violet, and you haven't exactly been nice to her." Jess pulled his arm away from

Violet when it became covered in the sugary punch. "What's on your costume, Violet?"

"Mallory spilled her punch on me." Violet left the hall to find some paper towels in the kitchen. She turned on the sink faucet, wet the paper towels, and attempted to save her costume.

Savannah stepped into the kitchen and grabbed a paper towel, surprising Violet by trying to help her. "Are you all right?" Savannah whispered.

Violet shook her head and blinked back tears.

Because of the open-concept style of the house, from the kitchen, Violet could still see Jess's eyes flash with anger. "Get out of here. Now," he growled at Mallory, pointing to the front door.

Mallory pouted and tried to act innocent. "It was just an accident. Do you really think I would do something like that on purpose?"

"You've treated Violet like shit for months. I didn't invite you to this party, so get out of my house now."

"That's all water under the bridge. Right, Violet?" Mallory asserted.

Violet stared at Mallory, staring in disbelief as she and Savannah dabbed at her costume with a wad of paper towels. "It's not, though. You've made my sophomore year of high school nearly unbearable. If it hadn't been for Jess and Kayla—well, I would be a lot worse off now. Jess is right. You should leave."

Mallory glared at both of them and stomped off, her friends following her obediently.

"Savannah! What are you doing? We're leaving," Mallory commanded from the doorway.

Savannah mouthed "sorry" at Violet as she scampered away too.

Jess turned to Violet and smiled. He took the paper towels from her and set them on the counter. She returned the smile, grateful that he had intervened, but crestfallen about how Mallory had tried to ruin the party.

"Do you think she'll really leave me alone now?" Violet asked hopefully.

Jess's lips turned down, and his smile vanished. "I don't know. At least for tonight, she should."

"How did she know about your party?" Violet asked, wondering if Jess had told Mallory. Or was she being paranoid? He wouldn't do that, right? He cared about her.

"She must have heard about the party from someone else in our grade. I invited a lot of people, in case you didn't notice." Jess grinned, gesturing around at the crowded room.

"She pulls off the Catwoman costume so much better than I do," Violet said with a resigned sigh as the image of Mallory in the skintight spandex suit flashed through her mind.

"What? Are you kidding me? You look amazing."

"I should probably figure out what to do about my costume, though. I don't think this is getting the stain out." Violet pointed to the soaking wet paper towels.

"Come on, let's go to my room. You can borrow some of my clothes."

Violet followed Jess downstairs to his bedroom, where he handed her a T-shirt and sweatpants. He was only a few inches taller than her, but she still knew she would look ridiculous in his clothes.

Before she could go to the bathroom to change her outfit, Jess pulled her tightly to him and wrapped his arms around her waist, embracing her. Apparently, he didn't care about the sticky punch all over her that much. Violet's entire body tingled at being so close to Jess. He had been so sweet to her for the entire night, thrown her a surprise party, and made sure Mallory couldn't ruin their night. He had even stood up to Mallory and told her to leave Violet alone. And it hadn't been the first time he had rescued her from Mallory. She thought back to the day they met in the cafeteria. How he had intervened after Izzy pushed her and everyone laughed at her.

Hadn't she punished Jess enough? Maybe she should get back together with him.

Jess bent down until his face was even with hers, pressing his lips gently against hers. She returned the kiss, wrapping her arms around his neck. He entangled his hands in her hair and deepened the kiss; her body molded against his.

"We should get back to the party," Violet said, smiling up at Jess.

She placed her hand in his and they left his room. They had barely moved down the hallway to head back upstairs when they spotted Kayla.

"We have a problem," Kayla said quietly, glancing back and forth between Jess and Violet. "My mom texted me. We need to speed up the plan and complete Part 1 as soon as possible. We need to kill Jimmy tonight," she said, her eyes blazing fiercely.

# Chapter 23:
# Before Jess

*September 13, 2019*

Violet had spent the weekend hanging out with Abby. Abby had flown into the tiny Asheville airport on Friday evening. Her flight landed at 6 p.m. Her parents had let her leave school early to visit Violet for the weekend. Violet's dad had talked to Abby's parents and decided it was for the best, and they all hoped it would help Violet's mental health. Jocelyn didn't protest when William told her Abby was visiting. He was the one doing all the grocery shopping and errands. Plus, he had already agreed to pick Abby up from the airport, so it didn't affect her.

When William told Violet they were going to the airport to pick up someone after school, she guessed it was Abby. Her dad smiled broadly when the two friends reunited. "It was worth it to see you happy like this again," he told them when they hugged.

Violet hugged her dad afterward, appreciating that he looked out for her wellbeing and did his best to cheer her up. But she also knew that letting Abby come stay with them was probably his way of not knowing what else to do or how to handle things. He hadn't tried talking to her about what was going on in-depth, especially after Jocelyn refused to let her switch to remote learning.

Violet and Abby spent the weekend catching up on everything going on in their lives. Abby talked endlessly about Scott, how much she missed Violet, and how different things were without Violet there. William chauffeured them around for the weekend. He dropped them off downtown and they strolled around Asheville, grabbed coffee and lunch at a café, shopped, went on a ghost-themed walking tour of the city, and spent part of a day hiking in the mountains. William sent Glenn with them on the hike though because he didn't like the thought of two young girls hiking in the mountains alone, especially since neither of them was very savvy with directions or navigating with a map. Glenn had been a Boy Scout for years and, despite his video game addiction, he didn't rely on his phone to get everywhere. He was the perfect guide for their little adventure. He surprised Violet by being patient with them when they kept stopping and asking him to take photos of them posing on the trail.

After the hike, Violet and Abby were exhausted and lounged in Violet's bedroom. It was Abby's last night in town. She was flying back to Michigan in the morning.

"I know we've been having a lot of fun the past few days and I'm really glad I came, but—" Abby started.

"What?" Violet asked, instantly sensing that the mood was killed. She knew what Abby was going to bring up.

"I wasn't sure if you wanted to talk about it, but I think we should. Are you *really* okay, Vi?"

"I'm fine." Violet busied herself with pretending to organize her desk, which was already immaculate.

"Well, you say that, but as much as I've enjoyed seeing you, I can tell you're not... doing well."

"Why did you have to ruin the weekend? Everything was going perfectly fine until now." Violet slammed the drawer of her desk, causing the framed picture of her and Abby to topple over.

Abby held up her hands in front of her body defensively. "I only want you to be happy. Your dad talked to my parents, and they let me come here because we're all worried about you. The thing is, you're not okay, Violet. Can you make some friends? Is there something I can do to help? Or maybe you could convince your parents to let you take online classes?"

"You can't help me. I've already tried everything I can think of, even online classes. My dad seemed fine with it, but my mom shot down the idea because she said I need to 'be more social,' which is fan-fucking-tastic when I'm being bullied and terrified to talk to anyone at school now."

Abby pursed her lips. "Could you transfer schools? I'm sure there's a private school in the area. You could finish out the semester and transfer in the spring."

"I wish, but my parents would never go for that. It would cut into my college tuition money that they've been saving for me."

Abby's eyes widened in shock and envy. "Wow, you're lucky your parents are going to pay for college for you. I'm not sure how I'm going to afford it yet or if I can even go."

Violet's angry face softened at Abby's plight. "I'm sorry. I didn't know that."

Abby shrugged as if it wasn't a big deal. "It's fine. I mean—it's not, but I've accepted it. I know you have a lot of awful things going on right now, but you're not the only one with problems," she said softly.

Violet's body posture stiffened, and she fought the suddenly overwhelming urge to cry. "You're right. I've been insensitive. You've been such a good friend to me. Listening to me complain all the time since I moved. Coming all the way here to cheer me up. I—I appreciate it all. I don't mean to sound ungrateful—"

Abby walked over to Violet and hugged her tightly. "No, it's fine. You're going through a lot. You have other things on your mind. We've stayed friends this long for a reason. We're always there for each other."

Violet nodded as tears slipped down her cheeks. She brushed the tears away. "Ugh, sorry. I'm so emotional lately."

"It's fine. I know it's been tough. Wanna watch a movie since it's my last night here?" Abby suggested, trying to change the subject to something lighter.

"Sure. You pick."

Violet and Abby spent the rest of the night curled up in Violet's bed watching movies, eating junk food, and chatting. At one point, Emilia knocked on the bedroom door and asked to join them, to which they happily agreed.

# Chapter 24:
# After Jess

*October 26, 2019*

Violet gaped at Kayla, wondering if she was serious. The party was still going on around them. The bass thumped from the speakers strategically wired throughout the house in the inconspicuous way only the wealthy could afford. She must have misheard her. She leaned in closer to Kayla.

"What?"

"Let's go talk in Jess's room," Kayla shouted, motioning for them both to follow her.

Violet and Jess complied. Jess entered his bedroom last and closed the door behind them, shutting out most of the noise from the party.

Violet looked at Jess, wondering if he was as thrown off as she was. "Fine. We can speed up the plans, for sure." Jess nodded as he paced across his bedroom.

"What plans?" Violet flopped onto Jess's bed, feeling drunk and hungry. She had never had a chance to eat all the food she had piled onto her plate earlier.

Kayla and Jess exchanged a look. "I think it's time we tell you everything. There are a few parts to our plan. Part 1 has to do with Jimmy," Kayla said.

Jess nodded again.

Kayla took a deep breath, held it for a few seconds, then exhaled loudly. Jess walked over to his large mahogany dresser and opened a drawer, digging around until he found what he was looking for and showed it to them triumphantly.

"Times like this call for whiskey!" Jess popped the cap off and took a gulp before passing it to Violet.

She had never tried whiskey, but she took a small sip and swallowed painfully. It burned her throat. She coughed, covered her mouth with her hand, and passed the bottle to Kayla. Kayla took a large swig and passed it back to Jess.

"Okay. My mom's boyfriend, Jimmy, has been around for a while. A few years now. At first, he seemed all right. Like most of her previous boyfriends, he wasn't an especially great guy, but he had a job and a car and he seemed to like my mom. All those things automatically made him better than half of her boyfriends. After a few months, though, I heard them fighting one night when he was staying over. He was screaming at my mom, and I mean *really*, screaming. She couldn't get a word in. I shut the basement door and stayed downstairs the rest of the night because I figured it would go down like it usually did with her boyfriends. He was pissed off about something and would break up with her. She would mope around the house for a few weeks, then bring home a different guy. But it wasn't like that with Jimmy."

Kayla stopped talking to catch her breath and gestured to the whiskey bottle that Jess held. "Pass me that."

Kayla sipped the whiskey and wiped her mouth with the back of her hand. Kayla continued, "It didn't take long after that before I realized he was abusive. This has been going on for years." She gripped the whiskey bottle tightly in her hands. "I told Jess what was going on because I didn't know if one day Jimmy would reach his breaking point and take things too far. I tried talking to my mom about it. More than once. She refused to admit anything was wrong. I knew I had to help her, but I wasn't sure how. Until Jess and I came up with our idea after his break-up last year." She looked at Jess and smiled sadly. "We were both at a low point, drinking late one night when his parents were out of town and we were hanging out here. I don't remember which one of us said it first, but we agreed it was the way to go. We wanted revenge on the people who hurt us. We wanted to make them pay for what they did to us. People can't just get away with treating other people like shit. It's not right," Kayla practically spat the words out as her anger became clear. Her eyes gleamed dangerously. "We need to kill Jimmy tonight," she echoed her earlier statement.

Jess grabbed the whiskey bottle from Kayla's hand and took a swig of the liquor. "So, what do you think, Violet? Are you with us?"

Her two friends stared back at her expectantly. Violet blurted out, "Of course," before she fully thought through her answer or the consequences. But she didn't think she would regret her decision. She might have been drunk, but she felt oddly clearheaded. She knew what she was getting into. And besides, Kayla was right. People like Jimmy shouldn't get away with treating people so badly. Kayla and her mom deserved better. Violet had seen the bruises on Kayla's throat and the fear on her friend's face. She could only imagine the horror that she and her mom had been through because of Jimmy. Violet was determined to help Kayla and Jess make sure Jimmy got what he deserved. No matter what it took to get there.

***

The trio went back upstairs to re-join the party, acting like everything was normal. They drank more, ate snacks, and danced until their feet were sore. By midnight, Jess was practically forcing people to leave his house. No one wanted the party to end, but they needed everyone to get out so they could focus on their plan.

After everyone left, they congregated in the kitchen. Violet and Kayla sat at the long, mahogany rectangular dining table, while Jess intermittently walked between the trays of food and picked over the remnants. It surprised Violet that he was still hungry, but he seemed to always be snacking on something.

"What do we need to do?" Violet asked them. "What's the first step in... taking him down?" She couldn't bring herself to say the words 'killing him.' If she didn't say it, maybe it wouldn't feel so wrong. Her mind went back and forth between wanting to kill Jimmy for what he did to Kayla and her mom and wanting to scream at Jess and Kayla that they were crazy for coming up with the idea. She wondered if they would follow through with it. They wouldn't, would they? *Her friends couldn't be murderers.*

Jess shoved more chips into his mouth and brushed crumbs off his fingers. "Kayla said Jimmy owns a gun that he carries with him everywhere. Supposedly, he has a concealed carry permit, but who knows if that's a lie? We need to get the gun from him and shoot him in the head—make it look like he committed suicide. He drinks a lot, so if he dies while he's drunk, the cops might think it was an accident."

Violet's mind whirled with the thought of shooting a man in the head and staging it to make it look like a suicide. "Who's going to shoot him?"

"I am," Kayla said determinedly. "I should be the one to do it. He's messed up my family."

"Won't the police be able to trace the gun for fingerprints?" Violet's voice quavered. She tried to think through all the details. They couldn't afford to miss anything if they were really going to do this.

"Not if we all wear gloves. We'll wear masks too, so Jimmy can't see our faces in case something goes wrong," Jess explained.

"Jimmy's at my house right now. My mom texted me and said that he's gone psychotic. Apparently, he came over already on a rampage. He screamed at her and threatened to kill her. I'm sure she believed him. He's capable of it. My mom was so scared that she locked herself in her bedroom. She told me not to come home tonight because she's worried about what he'll do if he sees me. But I can't leave her at home alone to fend for herself! I don't want something to happen to her. And I can't call the police because Jimmy would lose it if he knew I got law enforcement involved. This is our only option. My mom is all I have left for family," Kayla said tearfully.

Violet had never seen Kayla look so scared. She placed a comforting hand on Kayla's arm. "Don't worry. We'll make sure your mom is okay. We'll stop Jimmy so he can't ever hurt you or your mom again."

Jess looked at her and smiled approvingly, as if he was glad she had agreed to aid them in murder. This was *not* how she ever imagined her sixteenth birthday.

# Chapter 25:
# After Jess

*October 26, 2019*

Kayla was the most sober, so she drove the three of them to her house; although she still may have been a bit too intoxicated to legally drive, they made it to her house without any incidents. She drove slowly and followed all the traffic laws.

Jess had let Violet wear one of his dark hoodies, so she wore that over the borrowed T-shirt and sweatpants. She thought she looked like a dork wearing his baggy clothes, but Jess assured her she looked hot. Jess wore a nearly identical hoodie and gave one to Kayla also from his seemingly endless supply. Violet supposed it was because his parents were wealthy and could buy him as many of the same hoodie as he wanted.

They each wore gloves covering their hands and ski masks over their faces to conceal their identities. They didn't want Jimmy or Kayla's mom, Molly, to be able to identify them later. Although if they weren't able to kill Jimmy, Violet still thought he would assume Kayla or Molly was involved, especially if an attempt at murder occurred at Kayla's house. Who else would try to kill him while he was there?

They snuck into the house through the basement door, leaving it unlocked in case they needed a quick escape. Kayla thought it was best to leave her car parked down the street, so Jimmy didn't notice her car in the driveway. She didn't want him to be alerted to her presence. They needed to catch him off guard. Kayla told them he usually kept his gun in the glove compartment in his car, but if he was in a mood, he sometimes brought it into the house. Kayla said he always pulled it out when he was drunk and angry, threatening her and her mom if they pissed him off.

Jess peeked into the window of Jimmy's beaten-up looking truck. The glove compartment was closed, and he didn't see the gun from outside the car. Of course, the truck was locked. They hoped Jimmy had brought the gun into the house. Otherwise, there was always Plan B.

Once they were in the basement, Jess snuck up the stairs leading to the main floor of the house first. He slowly opened the door and looked around before beckoning for Kayla and Violet to follow him. Jess had a pocketknife in his hoodie pocket, just in case.

Jess stealthily crept through the hallway and into the kitchen, searching for the gun. Violet and Kayla followed closely behind him.

When they thought they wouldn't be able to find the gun, they heard an angry shout.

"Hey!" A man lumbered into the kitchen toward them. He wore a flannel shirt and gray sweatpants and deserved a 'most fashionable man of the year' award. "What are you doing in here? My girlfriend's got nothing to steal," Jimmy said, outraged.

At least he didn't know who they were. He thought they were burglars. *Good. Maybe this will be fine after all.*

Jess deepened his voice more than usual, imitating his Batman voice from earlier, doing his best to disguise himself. "Give us whatever you have. Money, your watch, any jewelry your girlfriend has—anything valuable," Jess demanded, going along with the ruse.

Jimmy calmly walked over to the front door, where a tall table stood with his gun resting on top of it. He picked it up and held it in his left hand. He stood in the hall in a cocky stance, his thick legs spread wide apart and shoulders set back. They hadn't had time to search the entire house yet and hadn't known the gun was there. *Damn it.*

Jimmy pointed the gun at Jess, perhaps deciding since he was the only one who spoke that he was the leader of the group. The one to take down. "You have ten seconds to get the fuck outta here," Jimmy said authoritatively, spittle flying from his mouth.

Jess stood protectively in front of Kayla and Violet and gestured for them to stay back. He pulled out his pocketknife and held it out in front of him. "I told you to give us anything valuable in this house," Jess said, his voice steely.

Violet wondered how he sounded so calm. She thought she would throw up in fear and anticipation of what would happen next. They had been so stupid to think they could do this. And now their lives were on the line. Why had she come with them? Why had she agreed to it? Because she hadn't thought they would go through with it.

Jimmy smirked. "What do you think you're going to do with that? And what kind of burglar goes into someone's house without a gun?" Jimmy suddenly surveyed the front door and entrance. "How did you get into the house, anyway?" Apparently, Jimmy wasn't as dumb as he looked.

"We got in through the basement. A broken latch on the window down there," Kayla said, her voice sounding hoarse.

Violet nodded along with Kayla's lie.

Jimmy waved the gun around irritably. "I don't need you messing up my night. My girlfriend's already in a pissy mood, and I guess that means no sex for me. But that doesn't mean I shouldn't get any fun tonight." He grunted and pulled the trigger on the gun.

Jess immediately shoved Kayla and Violet to the floor and ducked, the bullet narrowly missing his head. "Fuck!" he screamed as the bullet tore through the kitchen pantry.

With his arms shaking, Jess stood from his crouched position and screamed manically, launching himself at Jimmy. Jess wasn't particularly small, but he was only a teenager, and Jimmy was a big man. Jess attempted to shove Jimmy to the ground, but he didn't possess the strength to take down someone so much bigger than himself. However, the gun clattered from Jimmy's hand as he grappled with Jess and lost his grip on the gun.

Kayla shot forward, grabbing the gun and holding it in her right hand. She stood several feet away, trying to aim for Jimmy's head, but Jess was still wrestling with him, enduring sloppy punch after sloppy punch to his face, stomach, and chest as Jimmy pummeled him. Jimmy was clearly drunk and having trouble aiming his punches. Jess cried out when one of Jimmy's punches made direct contact with his nose, eliciting a terrible crunching sound that could have only meant Jess's nose was broken.

Kayla held the gun straight out in front of her. She pulled the trigger and the gunshot rang out, echoing across the dirty white tiles in the kitchen. Violet turned in horror to watch the bullet blow through its target, erupting a spray of blood onto the faded gray paint on the walls and further dirtying the tile flooring.

# Chapter 26:
# After Jess

*October 26, 2019*

"Fuck, fuck, fuck," Jess said as he tried to shove Jimmy's lifeless, heavy body off of him. "We have to get out of here."

Violet rushed over to help Jess stand, noticing that he winced as he gratefully took her hand. She wasn't sure how badly he was injured and if they needed to take him to the hospital. "Kayla?" she prompted.

Kayla stood in the same position, the gun dangling from her hand. She let the gun clatter to the floor. Violet picked it up with her gloves still on and strategically placed it in Jimmy's right hand.

"I need to check on my mom." Kayla headed to an area of the house that Violet hadn't seen yet. She assumed the hall led to her mom's bedroom, where she was supposedly hiding out.

Violet grabbed Kayla's arm to pull her back. "No! She can't see you. Your mom can't know that we were involved. Remember?"

"Uh, guys, I don't think we need to worry about that. Wouldn't your mom have heard the gunshot?" Jess asked as he looked at Kayla.

Kayla's face paled. "Good point. We should leave in case she comes out to investigate or calls the police." She wildly scanned her eyes around the kitchen. "Is there any evidence we need to get rid of?"

Jess eyed Jimmy's prone body with disdain. "We all had gloves on while we were here and Jimmy's fingerprints should be all over the gun. It should be a straightforward case. The police will assume he killed himself. Let's get out of here."

Violet was already bounding down the basement steps, eager to leave the crime scene and return to her safe home. Kayla and Jess joined her outside shortly after. Kayla locked the basement door behind them.

Soon, the trio was back at Jess's house. Kayla and Violet had each texted their parents to say that a bunch of them were crashing at Jess's house for the night. Violet's mom had protested at first, but reluctantly gave in. They had decided it was for the best if the three of them remained together for the night. Just in case.

***

*October 27, 2019*

The next morning, Violet awoke in an unfamiliar bed. She groggily gazed at her surroundings until she remembered she had stayed the night at Jess's house. And apparently slept in his bed with him. He snored loudly next to her, one of his arms curled around her waist. She nestled into his chest and tried to get comfortable again, but groaned when she thought about last night. She had tossed and turned for hours before becoming so exhausted that she must have fallen asleep. She didn't know how Jess had managed to sleep peacefully after what they had done. *Didn't it bother him?*

Violet shook Jess, unable to sleep anymore.

"Ungh," he groaned. "What time is it?" he asked, with his eyes still closed.

Violet yanked the blanket off of him. "Wake up, it's almost 9 a.m."

Jess grabbed the blanket from her and tugged it back over his body.

"Way too early," Jess mumbled, pulling her close to him.

A knock came from the bedroom door.

Violet extricated herself from Jess's embrace and let him talk to Kayla, while she went into Jess's private bathroom. Violet was wearing one of Jess's T-shirts still, but she had been so tired that she hadn't removed her makeup before going to bed. Her face was a smeared mess.

She opened a few cabinets until she found a washcloth to clean her face and wiped off the smudged makeup. After she freshened up, she returned to his bedroom and realized Jess and Kayla weren't there anymore. She wandered down the hall and found them in the kitchen, scrounging around for breakfast.

Kayla smiled wearily when she saw her. "Morning, Violet."

"Morning," Violet replied, sitting at the table.

"Have either of you checked the news yet?" Jess held his phone in his hand and peered at it intently.

They both shook their heads.

He abandoned the skillet on the stove where he had been frying eggs and placed his phone on the table where they could see it.

*Asheville, NC: Middle-aged man discovered dead in his girlfriend's house late last night. There were no witnesses. He appears to have died from a self-inflicted gunshot wound to the head. The investigation is ongoing.*

"That's good, right? That means the police don't suspect someone killed him?" Violet nervously bit her lip.

Kayla's gleeful smile vanished from her face. "I didn't think there would be an investigation. What if we missed something? What if they find out what we did?"

Jess took his phone back and walked over to the stove to watch the eggs. "No, our back-up if they found out we were involved is to say that it was self-defense. We're just kids. They won't suspect us of doing something like this. It will be fine."

"How do you know that for sure, though?" Kayla's worried tone reflected Violet's thoughts.

As Violet thought about the investigation and what they had done last night, the scent of frying eggs filled the kitchen and invaded her nostrils. She gagged and ran to the bathroom in the hallway, narrowly making it to the toilet before whiskey, party punch, and the snacks she had consumed last night erupted from her mouth. After several more heaves, she laid down on the cool bathroom tiles, cradling her head in her hands.

Kayla came into the bathroom. "Are you okay?" She bent down and handed her a glass of water.

Violet sipped it gratefully. "Thanks." She drank half of the water and set it down on the floor. "No, I'm not okay. What if we get caught?"

Kayla fixed her with a hard gaze and turned to leave the bathroom. "Just listen to Jess. We didn't do anything wrong. It was self-defense. We didn't have a choice."

The Quiet Girl

suffer. That was the last thing she wanted her parents to complain about.

Violet's parents still didn't know about Jess, and she preferred to keep it that way. They would be livid if they found out she had stayed the night with her boyfriend and slept in the same bed as him.

While she worked on a particularly difficult geometry problem, her sister barged into her room, closed the door promptly, and sat down on Violet's bed, leaning forward in earnest.

"Can I help you?" Violet asked with a solemn look on her face.

Emilia grinned. "You spent the night at Jess's house. And he threw a surprise birthday party for you! I'm jealous. *That's so sweet.* Are you guys back together now? Do you love him? Do you think you'll marry him?"

Violet laughed at Emilia's questions. Sometimes it was easy to forget her sister was two years younger than her, but other times, her age showed. She shrugged, attempting to appear nonchalant. "We're just dating. I like him a lot, though."

"Is he a good kisser?" Emilia hugged one of Violet's fuzzy throw pillows to her chest.

"He's an amazing kisser. None of my other boyfriends made me feel like this," Violet admitted.

Emilia giggled. "I knew it! Do Mom and Dad know?" Her expression sobered slightly.

"No, and please don't mention it to them. They'll probably flip out if they know. And they definitely wouldn't have let me stay at his house if they knew we were dating."

"True." Emilia cocked her head to the side. "Does that mean you, like, slept with him?"

"We slept in the same bed together, if that's what you mean." Violet's cheeks flamed as she looked away from her sister and stared out the window. It wasn't a lie. Nothing had happened.

"Oh, fiiine. Don't tell me all the sordid details. I'm just living vicariously through you until I have a hot boyfriend."

Violet shook her head. "Don't grow up too fast, Em. Enjoy being young."

Emilia rolled her eyes and dropped the pillow, scrolling through her phone while she lounged on Violet's bed. She gasped as her eyes flitted over something on her phone. She looked like she was reading something.

"What?" Violet assumed Emilia was looking at a meme or reading the latest celebrity gossip.

"Did you hear about the guy who was found dead this morning? Apparently, his girlfriend called the police because they had a fight. The police rushed to her house and found his body. They're assuming it was suicide, but haven't confirmed the cause of death yet, so he could have been murdered. It happened in Asheville, not far away. That's so creepy!" Emilia shuddered.

Violet's face blanched, and she nearly dropped the pen she had been clutching in her hand. "Wh-what?" she stammered. "No, I didn't hear about it. That's awful."

"Yeah, the article I just read said he was dating someone whose daughter attends your school. The article didn't mention any names, though. Any idea who it could be?"

Violet shook her head fervently. "Nope, no clue," she said quickly. "Sorry, Em, can you leave? I have a lot of homework due tomorrow."

Emilia's face fell. "You never have time for me anymore now that you have Jess and Kayla. I was there for you when you needed me and now you can't even spare an hour for me. You're such a bitch!" She stormed off, slamming Violet's bedroom door as she left before Violet could form a response.

Her sister's theatrics slightly surprised her, but she was used to it. Emilia could be emotional if she didn't get what she wanted. She hoped Emilia would cool off if she left her alone for a few hours. Her sister being mad at her was just what she needed. Yet another thing to worry about in her life that was spiraling out of control once again. But this time, she was wrapped up in something more dangerous than ever. This time, it was life or death.

# Chapter 28: After Jess

*October 28, 2019*

On Monday, everyone at the high school obsessed over the man who had been found dead over the weekend. The police didn't seem to be pointing fingers at anyone yet, nor had they brought anyone in for questioning, but it was still early in the process, and Violet knew they weren't safe yet. She hoped Jess and Kayla would forget about whatever the rest of their plan entailed, so she could focus on being a normal teenager for once.

When Violet met up with Kayla and Jess during their lunch period, she wondered how to broach the subject. She didn't know if it was a good idea to talk about what they did over the weekend while they were at school and anyone could overhear their conversation. But she also wasn't sure that she wanted to be involved in anything else illegal or dangerous. She realized that might affect her relationship with Jess—but she would worry about that later.

Jess sat on the bench next to her at their usual table, setting down two trays fully laden with food and passing one to her. "Here. I got you lunch."

Violet smiled appreciatively. "Thanks."

Kayla was silent, intently staring at her phone. Her face looked pale and practically drained of all color, making her purple hair stand out even more than usual in comparison.

"You okay?" Jess eyed Kayla with concern.

Kayla placed her phone on the table and put her head in her hands, groaning as she did so.

"Reading those news articles about what happened this weekend?" Jess guessed.

Kayla nodded with her head still in her hands and after a moment, finally sat up and looked at them. "I've read every article I could find. I really hope they deem it a suicide soon and don't investigate the possibility of homicide."

"Won't they want to interview you anyway, since your mom dated him?" Violet asked with a sudden realization.

"Shit, you're probably right. We're so screwed," Kayla responded, fixing her purple hair into a messy ponytail, so it was out of her face.

Jess pushed his fries toward Kayla. "You didn't get any food? Have some of mine. You need to eat."

"I'm not hungry." Kayla glanced at the fries with disgust. Her phone lit up with a text notification. She read the text, and Violet and

Jess waited impatiently for her to tell them whether it was related to Jimmy.

"It's my mom. She said the Asheville Police Department called her at work and asked her to come in for questioning."

Violet didn't think it was possible, but Kayla's complexion seemed paler. She gently patted Kayla's arm. "We're here for you. We'll get through this."

Kayla tugged on her ponytail anxiously. "I know. My mom said they asked to question me after school today too. She has to be with me when I'm questioned, since I'm a minor. I can't believe this is happening."

Violet refrained from saying, *what did you think was going to happen after you murdered your mom's boyfriend?* Instead, she played the role of the comforting friend. After all, she was wrapped up in this mess too. She didn't know for sure if she could go to jail for being involved in the murder, but she assumed it was a possibility. They had planned the murder ahead of time. It's not like she couldn't have tried to stop Kayla and Jess from enacting their twisted plan. But then again, what would she have done? She would lose her only friends, not to mention her boyfriend, if she spoke out against them. Was that what she wanted? Jimmy was a terrible person—absolute scum who abused Kayla and her mom for far too long—and they had stopped him permanently. Wasn't that a good thing? She had to convince herself it had been the right decision or she would go mad.

"Do you want to go over what you're going to tell the police?" Jess prompted quietly. "We need to make sure we all have the same story in case we get questioned too."

They spent the rest of their lunch period making sure they were all on the same page about how the weekend went. Jess's party provided the perfect alibi—they had been at his house all night with dozens of witnesses who could vouch for them being there. Kayla hadn't gone home until the next afternoon and presumably no one had witnessed them entering Kayla's house. They had taken every precaution to make sure they wouldn't be caught. And they wouldn't be, as long as they all stuck to the story.

\*\*\*

Violet sipped her iced coffee gratefully. She needed a caffeine boost after the day she had. She was at Big Beanz with Jess. Kayla was at the Asheville Police Department with her mom. She had driven there directly after school. Violet and Jess were hanging out at the coffee shop until Kayla was done with her questioning, then they planned to meet up with her later to see how it went. Hopefully with no issues.

Violet had trouble concentrating on her homework, especially when Jess kept gazing at her from across the table.

"How am I supposed to get anything done with you staring at me like that?" she asked him with a playful smirk.

Jess shrugged one shoulder and helped himself to the plate of cookies his mom had brought over to them earlier. The plate was now half-empty, thanks to Jess. Sometimes Violet wondered how someone who seemed to always be eating didn't gain weight.

"It's not my fault that I'm distracting. It's both a pleasure and a curse."

"A pleasure for who?" Violet retorted.

Jess pretended to be wounded and grabbed her geometry textbook to see what she was struggling with. "I can help you with this. I took geometry last year."

Violet's mouth practically dropped open. "All this time I've been struggling, and you never thought to mention you're good at math?" She lightly hit him on the shoulder, but he held onto her hand and pressed his lips against it.

She sighed happily before pulling her hand away. "Okay, stop goofing around. Help me figure out this equation."

\*\*\*

By the time 6 p.m. rolled around, Violet felt a headache forming from focusing on math for so long. Of course, there had been intermittent breaks with kissing and cuddling Jess—and eating way too many homemade cookies—but she never wanted to look at a math equation again.

Kayla entered the coffee shop. Before she sat down at the table with them, Violet stood and anxiously grabbed Kayla's arm.

"Is everything okay?" Violet asked.

Kayla pulled Violet's arm off and sank into the chair next to Violet. "I'm exhausted. I followed our plan, though. They said they might need to talk to both of you, since we were together the whole night."

"That's fine; we have nothing to hide," Jess responded.

Violet gave him a look that implied he was crazy.

"What?" Jess asked innocently, putting his arm around Violet.

"Never mind. Hopefully that's the end of it," Violet said.

Jess leaned in close to both of them to whisper, so no one would hear them talking. "What about Part 2 of our Big Bad Plan?"

Violet gritted her teeth. She had dreaded this conversation, but she remained silent, waiting for Kayla's reaction.

"I don't know, Jess. Maybe we should wait until the police have moved on from the case before we... you know..." Kayla said hesitantly, avoiding eye contact with Jess.

Jess slammed his hands down on the table. "That wasn't part of our plan," he said through clenched teeth. "You promised you would uphold your part in this if I helped you with Jimmy!"

Kayla shrank away from Jess. "Calm down. We don't want anyone to hear us talking about this in here. And don't mention his fucking name in public."

Jess ran his hands roughly through his curly brown hair, as if he was holding back his anger. "Fine, we won't talk about it now, but you're going to help me, Kayla. Because if you don't, I'll go to the police and tell them what you did. I'll tell them you killed him."

# Chapter 29:
# After Jess

*October 28, 2019*

Even though it was a school night, Violet convinced her parents to let Kayla stay the night. Now that Jimmy was out of the picture, Kayla was safe at her home, but her mom was still a mess because of what happened, and Kayla said she was tiring to be around. Kayla hadn't considered that if her mom thought her boyfriend had committed suicide, she would blame herself for not stopping him. Kayla felt guilty for contributing to her mom's emotional state and kept reiterating to Violet that what they did was the right decision. Violet assumed it was Kayla's way of trying to cope with the guilt.

"You feel guilty too, don't you?" Kayla interrupted Violet's thoughts.

An old Batman movie played on the TV in Violet's bedroom, but neither of them paid attention to it. It was only playing as a distraction and to cover the sound of their conversation in case any of Violet's family members walked by her room and overheard something they shouldn't.

Violet hesitated, but she didn't want to lie to Kayla. Despite the craziness of what they had done, Kayla was her friend. She breathed in deeply and exhaled, trying to expel her anxiety from her body. "Yeah, of course I feel guilty. We killed someone. Even if he deserved it."

Kayla nodded solemnly. "Jess doesn't seem to have an issue with it. I guess that's his way of dealing with what we did. Acting like it was the only choice we had."

"I think so." Violet paused, unsure how to bring up the topic, but knowing this was the perfect opportunity to talk to Kayla about it while the two of them were alone, without Jess around. "What exactly is Part Two of your plan with Jess? Or do I not want to know?"

Kayla fidgeted with the hem of her baggy rock band T-shirt before she answered Violet. "No, I'll tell you. Since you know about his history with Mallory, you know how much he hates her. I'm still not sure why he texted her a few weeks ago. He wants revenge on her. Just like you do. The next part of the plan has to do with that. We have some... dirt on her family that would ruin their reputation."

"What? How did you find out something like that?"

"Since Jess's parents own the coffee shop and it's become such a popular hangout for locals, everyone is always there—for dates, business meetings, casual meals with their families, whatever—and it's not exactly a discrete place to meet."

"Yeah? What does that have to do with Mallory's family?" Violet wondered where the conversation was headed.

"Her dad is having an affair with Izzy's mom," Kayla blurted out quickly and broke her eye contact with Violet.

"What?! Oh my God." Violet's stomach twisted at the shocking secret.

Kayla continued explaining. "We saw them at Big Beanz over the summer. I followed them out to the parking lot and acted like I was getting something from my car. I saw them making out in his car." She shuddered at the memory. "Like, he was *all* over her. I don't know why they did that in public where anyone could see them. I guess they thought no one was watching, and I was the only other person in the parking lot. Or maybe they didn't care who saw them. Either way, I took pictures for potential blackmail. I knew it would be useful."

"Won't Izzy be upset when she finds out? This affects her too." Violet picked at her nails. She didn't know Izzy very well, and she had never been nice to Violet, but she felt sorry for her after what she had just heard.

Kayla shoved a few potato chips into her mouth from the large bowl perched on Violet's desk. "It's a necessary casualty. She's friends with Mallory, so she's fair game in this war. She goes along with all of her shit, so she deserves the backlash from Mallory's enemies."

Violet twisted her light brown hair around her finger. "So, after you reveal the news about the affair to everyone, then what?"

Kayla's face twisted into a devious smile. "Part Two of the plan has been in the works for a long time. We want to get back at Mallory for everything she's done—to Jess, to you, to everyone—and that's no small feat. Every year, Mallory and her entire family take part in this huge charity thing in downtown Asheville. They raise a ton of money for the homeless and try to make their family look good, despite all the shady things Mallory's dad is involved with. Money talks in this town, like it does in most places."

"What are you planning?" Violet asked. She needed to know what was going on. Maybe it wasn't too late to stop them.

"Well, the next part is supposed to happen at the charity event. It's next weekend. We're going to spread the news about Mallory's dad and Izzy's mom's affair. Mallory's dad is a powerful force in Asheville, so gossip like that, especially since it's true, will knock him down a few pegs. It should make him lose some of his influence. I'm sure it will take him a while to recover from it. Plus, it will reveal how slimy their whole family is and affect what everyone thinks about Mallory. Mallory cheated on Jess, so clearly having no self-control runs in her blood."

"Hmm. Are you sure that's the right move? Jess is fine with all of this?" Violet stretched out her legs on the bed as she pondered the plan.

Kayla shrugged, eating more of the chips. "It was Jess's idea. He's all for it."

"Are you going to go along with whatever he wants to do? Even if it's… dangerous?"

Kayla set down the chip bowl and brushed her crumb-covered hands across her sweatpants. "I've known Jess a lot longer than you. He would do anything for the people he cares about, and he's been a good friend to me. But if you cross him, he'll do everything in his power to destroy you like he plans on doing to Mallory."

"Would he really turn you into the police?" Violet asked, exasperated at the thought of Jess betraying Kayla when all of this was his master plan. Without him, none of this would have happened.

Kayla looked at her dead-on, her eyes completely serious. "I'm not sure, Violet, and that thought terrifies me. We have to do whatever he says, okay? If we don't, he's going to take us down."

"What if we come up with a plan of our own? What if I had a way to stop him?"

# Chapter 30:
# After Jess

*November 2, 2019*

Violet tugged down her dark gray sweater she had borrowed from her sister. It fit snugly, and she felt uncomfortable wearing such a form-fitting shirt. She had paired it with dark jeans and a pair of black combat boots. She figured if Jess forced her and Kayla to be a part of his crazy plan, then she might as well dress the part of a badass. If only she had the fighting skills of Catwoman, then she could really play the part.

She scanned the crowded downtown area for Kayla. Her distinctive purple hair was usually easy to spot. When she found Kayla, she joined her and they waited for Jess. They were going through with the next part of Jess's plan, so he didn't become suspicious and think they were turning on him. They wanted him on their side. Violet was nervous about continuing to date him and acting like everything was fine, but she didn't see another way out of it. He had threatened Kayla, and he was clearly dangerous. She didn't know how she would get out of the mess she found herself in, but she knew all wasn't lost yet.

Jess stepped up to where Violet and Kayla hung out near one of the many coffee shops downtown. He gave Violet a quick peck on the cheek. "Hey."

In return, she smiled and turned her face so they could kiss properly.

Nerves tingled throughout her body, and she decided she would need Kayla's help to make sure she didn't have to be alone with Jess. She was unsure how well she could hold up the charade without other people around to distract him. And she certainly didn't want to have to keep kissing someone who was planning on murdering multiple people.

"Are you guys ready for this?" Jess scanned the crowded area. His eyes were wild as he searched for Mallory and her family.

Violet and Kayla both nodded obediently.

"This is going to be the perfect revenge against that bitch for everything she's done—all the terrible things she's gotten away with. Mallory needs to be taught a lesson. When she broke up with me, she didn't know who she was messing with. She thought I would continue with my life and let her get away with what she did. Well, she was wrong," Jess monologued feverishly.

Violet barely recognized the boy she had a crush on for weeks, the person she cared about, the one who rescued her from her bullies and brought her so much happiness. When had he become so obsessed with vengeance? What had led Jess to become this way?

Kayla spoke up, "Everything is in place, so we should be all set. Before I met up with Violet, I texted Savannah and told her about the affair. I sent her the pictures I took also. I bought a burner phone, so she won't know it was me. The whole town will know by the time the festival is underway."

"Good thing she can't keep her mouth shut. Tonight, it will be all anyone can talk about." Jess chuckled and wrapped his arm securely around Violet's waist and pulled her closer to him.

Arms that she had once found comfort in now felt restricting— more like shackles than a safety net. Violet fought the urge to shove Jess's arms away from her. Instead, she grinned up at him.

"We might as well enjoy the festival while we're here, right? Let's go check out the events for this year." Jess tugged Violet along to follow him.

"What exactly is this festival for?" Violet asked as she allowed Jess to pull her down the street.

Kayla rolled her eyes. "Basically an excuse for all the wealthy people to look good and make themselves feel like they're contributing to the 'less fortunate' people of Asheville. This year, their fundraiser is focusing on the homeless, which, as I'm sure you've noticed, is a huge problem here." She gestured around vaguely, but she was right. There were always homeless people milling around the city. "There will be street vendors, food trucks, and a raffle. All the money raised will go toward the homeless shelter. Supposedly. Who knows if that's what they actually do with the money?"

The three teenagers wandered through the streets, checking out the street vendors who were already set up. Many of them had been there since early in the morning to prepare for the festival. There were way too many booths selling handmade jewelry, most of which looked like it would fall apart the second it was purchased. There was a caricature artist who looked interesting. A multitude of crafts being sold. And used books on display from the grand bookstore that was a focal point of the town. Violet gravitated to the books, happily flicking through the display as Jess watched her with amusement.

"Pick out whatever you want." He brandished a credit card from his wallet.

"What? Are you sure?" she asked with trepidation.

"Yeah, my parents gave me a credit card when I was like twelve. As long as I don't max it out every month, they don't care what I spend. Treat yo self, girl," he said with an impish grin.

Kayla stood off to the side, probably bored and not interested in Violet's book obsession.

Violet shot her an apologetic look. "Sorry, it's been a while since I've been to a bookstore. Just give me a few minutes. That's all I need!" she promised.

After Violet had carefully selected three books with potential and Jess had paid for them, they continued strolling through the festival. They stopped at a booth selling coffee. Violet ordered an iced coffee, despite the chilly November air whipping around them.

"You're crazy to be ordering a cold drink," Kayla teased her.

Violet shrugged, unbothered by the comment. "I'm from Michigan. Michiganders will eat ice cream outside in the winter too." She sipped her iced coffee as if to emphasize her point.

"Okay, craaazy," Kayla repeated, holding her steaming cup in her gloved hands as she tried to warm herself.

They continued walking around until they thought they had seen everything for the festival. All three of them entered the raffle and made a small donation to the charity. Jess stood as tall as possible, maximizing his 5-foot 9 height to see over the crowd of people.

"What are you looking for?" Violet asked.

"Mallory. I want to see the look on her face when the news breaks. She's going to be devastated." He grinned evilly.

He tightened his grip on her hand and they crossed the street to an area that appeared to be less populated.

"Maybe we can get a better view from here." Jess surveyed the area, his eyes scanning for Mallory.

Violet and Kayla surreptitiously exchanged a look.

Kayla shivered as a sudden gust of wind rustled the bare branches on the trees nearby. She pulled her coat closer around her body and zipped it all the way up to her chin. "God, it's fucking cold. Can we go inside somewhere for a while?"

Jess shook his head. "We need to stay outside so we know when it happens."

"I'm cold too. Kayla and I will go inside and wait," Violet said. An angry look crossed Jess's face, and she quickly added, "Just for a bit, okay?"

Kayla turned around to head to a coffee shop and Violet chased after her. Once they were inside and miraculously managed to snag an empty table, Kayla peered around the coffee shop.

"He didn't follow us, did he?" Kayla asked in a paranoid tone.

"I don't think so. We already had coffee earlier. Should we get some pastries while we're here?"

Kayla agreed and Violet waited in line to order muffins. She ordered an extra one for Jess, knowing he would be hungry because he was constantly snacking. She needed to stay on his good side.

Violet and Kayla munched on their muffins in silence. The noises of people chatting, laughing, and enjoying the festival floated around them. They were enjoying their reprieve from Jess.

"Do you think he'll be able to find Mallory?" Kayla asked.

"I'm not sure. What do you think he'll do if he finds her?" Violet polished off the rest of her lemon poppyseed muffin and rolled up the wrapper, tearing it into tiny pieces as her anxiety bubbled up inside her.

"Good question. Maybe we should find him so he doesn't do anything stupid."

"Is it bad that I'm scared to go back out there?"

Kayla smiled sympathetically. "We're in this together. Don't worry, I won't leave you alone with him."

"Thanks. I just hope we can make it through the day in one piece."

***

By the time Violet and Kayla rejoined the festivalgoers, whispers circulated throughout the streets. They found Jess standing nearby after a few minutes of searching.

"What's going on?" Violet asked him. "Is it the gossip about the affair?"

Jess smiled devilishly. "Yup, from what I can hear, that's what everyone's talking about right now. We did it!" He reached out his hand for a high five to Kayla and she reluctantly returned the high five. "Next step: take down Mallory for good."

"Uh… what exactly do you mean by that?" Violet asked.

"We can't talk about it in public. It's not safe. Should we go to our secret spot to discuss the next move?" Jess replied, looking at each of his friends.

"Sure," Kayla said before Violet could say anything.

"Okay," Violet said next. It's not like she had a choice.

# Chapter 31: After Jess

*November 2, 2019*

Kayla drove them to their secret spot, which Violet had only been to once before. She hadn't been back since they had first befriended her and let her glimpse their dark sides. So much had changed since then. She settled into a spot on one of the gnarled branches of the large tree, which stood barren above them. Jess sat in the middle, in between the two girls.

Violet cleared her throat, wondering what the next part of the plan involved. She could only hope it didn't involve murder. Kayla had hinted at that to her previously, but Violet didn't want to believe that Jess would really try to kill Mallory. She still hoped he was going through something, something that had messed him up. She hoped it wasn't permanent. Violet wanted him to snap out of it before things went any further—that he would go back to being the sweet, caring person he had been that day he rescued her from her bullies. Was that too much to hope for? Probably.

"Mallory's sixteenth birthday party is next weekend. Her parents own a cabin in the mountains. It's ridiculous—she took me there a few times when we were dating—it's more like a mansion than a cabin. Tons of bedrooms, at least two acres of land, a giant hot tub, very secluded—the perfect setting for a party. But even better, the perfect setting for a murder," Jess explained as his lips curled up into a sinister smile.

Violet gasped. "You don't want to—"

"What? Do you suddenly not want revenge on the bitch who tried to ruin your life? Mallory made you miserable for months. You can't lie to me, Violet. I know exactly how you feel, and I know you want her to pay. The only way to get back at her is to kill her. She doesn't deserve to live after what she did. Why should she be the one who gets to keep on living her perfect little life?" Jess wrapped his arm around Violet.

Goosebumps formed on her arm touching Jess, and it wasn't from the chill in the woods. It was from the cold look on her boyfriend's face as he talked about killing another person. Hadn't one death been enough? Why did they have to kill Mallory? Sure, she was awful, but Violet didn't think she deserved to die. No one did. She was regretting ever mentioning the idea to Jess, although she didn't know if that would have changed Jess's mind. Apparently, he had wanted revenge on Mallory long before she had met him.

"Jess is right, Violet," Kayla said with a meaningful look at her. "We need to finish the plan."

Violet sighed exasperatedly and wrapped her arms around her knees, pushing Jess's arm off. She didn't know how she would get out of this mess. "Okay, so we crash her sixteenth birthday party. Then what? How do we kill Mallory?"

Jess smirked and squeezed Violet's shoulder. "Not just Mallory. Don't you want revenge on all the people who wronged you? It wasn't just her; all her friends joined in. They tried to turn the entire school against you. If it wasn't for us, you wouldn't have made any friends." He stopped talking when he noticed the sour expression on Violet's face. "Sorry, I didn't mean it like that. I just meant—she won't stop until she destroys you, especially now that she knows we're together. She sees everything as a competition, and she doesn't want to lose. The fact that I didn't want to get back together with her really pissed her off."

"So, is the plan still the same, then?" Kayla asked calmly as she bit her fingernail. Her actions betrayed her genuine emotions. Violet knew she was pretending too.

"Yup," Jess said with a smile that chilled Violet. "We'll poison the drinks at Mallory's party and make it look like it was a mass suicide."

"Uh, how are we going to do that? What if we get caught?" Violet immediately asked, thinking he couldn't be serious. How did he think they could get away with something like that? If a hundred kids all died at a party, local law enforcement wouldn't just let it go. It wasn't a single death that they could frame, like with Jimmy.

"Trust me, Violet, we've been planning this for a while," Jess replied, squeezing her shoulder again. "I promise I'll take care of everything. I would never let something bad happen to you. Never again." His eyes glinted dangerously.

Violet looked toward Kayla, whose eyes were full of fear.

Violet trembled and tried to remain calm, since Jess's arm was still around her. She didn't want to reveal how truly terrified she was. If he thought something was off, who knew what he would do to her? She needed to stop Jess before he tried to kill half the students in their grade.

# Chapter 32: After Jess

*November 9, 2019*

Violet stalked through the woods, peering around every tree as she cautiously approached the cabin. She wore a sparkly purple dress that fell to her knees; it had a full skirt made of tulle that accentuated her hips and tiny waist. Her light brown hair was sleek and straightened. Emilia had helped apply her makeup and lined her eyes fiercely with eyeliner. She wore a purple sparkly masquerade mask that covered the top half of her face. Leave it to Mallory to want her sixteenth birthday party to be a masquerade party in a cabin in the woods. Violet needed to look the part to blend in, but despite her fancy outfit, she still donned her black combat boots. She wasn't a high heels kind of girl.

If Kayla had followed their plan, then she should be in position by now. Violet was unsure where Jess was and the thought worried her, but she was also fairly certain that he wouldn't hurt her. He liked her too much, in his own twisted way, and she didn't think he would risk losing her at this point. Violet couldn't let herself think about what she would do about him after all this was over. She couldn't stay with him. There had to be a way to break up with him that wouldn't make him want to kill her too.

As Violet followed the lantern-lit trail leading to Mallory's parents' large cabin, she heard a bloodcurdling scream and stopped walking, ducking behind a tree. Her heart thudded violently, and she put her hand to her chest, taking a few deep breaths. The cabin was close now. She pulled her cellphone out of her purse and swiped up to check her notifications. She needed to make sure Kayla was all right. There weren't any notifications on her phone.

She quickly clicked the phone icon next to Kayla's name and pressed her phone to her ear, feeling like the phone call took longer than usual to go through. Maybe it was the crappy cell phone service this high in the mountains. The cabin was secluded, and there probably wasn't a cell tower close by. Shit. She hadn't considered that possibility beforehand. What if she couldn't get hold of Kayla?

The phone stopped ringing, and a voice answered. "Violet..." Kayla's voice was so soft that Violet could barely hear her. "Help."

"What's wrong? Are you ok—" Violet started to say, but the call ended. She stared hopelessly at her phone for a moment before springing into action.

"FUCK."

Violet flung her phone into her purse and sprinted toward the cabin, no longer taking heed of any onlookers. She needed to save Kayla. She didn't know what had happened, but if Jess was with her, then she was in trouble. He had threatened to turn her into the police when he thought Kayla wouldn't cooperate, but neither Violet nor Kayla had thought Jess would hurt them. They still thought he cared deeply enough about them to not do anything extreme. But what else could have happened? If he found out that Violet and Kayla had been implementing a plan of their own, then he wouldn't be happy about it.

When she reached the front yard of the cabin, she slowed down. If Jess had caught Kayla, then she was probably inside the cabin. Dozens of teenagers dressed in formal attire and masquerade masks danced to the pop music blaring from the outdoor speakers. There was a keg in the yard and an enormous cooler full of mini liquor bottles. She didn't see any food, but she assumed it was inside the cabin; although she didn't think she could eat even if she wanted to with the nausea currently swimming in her stomach.

Violet entered the cabin tentatively and shut the front door behind her. There were a few people inside the cabin who she smiled at and waved to as she kept an eye out for Kayla or Jess, but most people mingled outside, drinking and dancing. Mallory probably didn't want many people inside the cabin.

As she entered the family room and scanned the area, she noticed two girls making out on one of the leather couches and hastily exited the room. Where could Kayla be? It would have been a lot easier to find her if she knew her way around the cabin, but she didn't. They weren't even supposed to be at Mallory's party. It's not like Mallory had invited them. She didn't want anyone to recognize her and be able to pin her as someone who had attended the party, especially if Jess had done something bad… something that could get them into trouble for being accomplices. That is, if Kayla was still alive.

Violet walked down the hall and knocked on a door, assuming it was a bedroom and wondering if people were having sex in there. It seemed likely. It was a party and most people were already drunk this late into the night. Nothing like cheap beer and a sixteenth birthday party at a cabin in the woods to make teenagers want to take off their clothes.

No one answered, so she opened the door. It was empty. She knocked on the next door, which turned out to be a bathroom. It looked like there were several more rooms upstairs, so she quickly ascended the stairs, her combat boots thudding with each step on the wooden stairs. Now wasn't the time to worry about being stealthy. She needed to find Kayla before it was too late.

She pounded her fists on each of the doors, one after the other. Two of the upstairs bedrooms had couples in them, but Violet didn't note who they were because they were wearing masks covering their faces and they didn't even glance at her as she opened the door. She mumbled awkward apologies as she closed the door.

Violet reached the final door, which she assumed led to Mallory's bedroom. Violet tentatively opened the door and stepped inside. At first glance, the room appeared empty. The light was off, so Violet flicked it on, illuminating a queen-sized bed with a wrinkled blue quilt.

Someone had been sitting on it recently.

"Hello? Is anyone in here?" She stepped further into the room. She barely noticed a black mask with silver swirls on the floor that was splattered with blood.

"Help..." a weak voice answered.

Violet raced into the ensuite bathroom. "Kayla? Is that you?"

"Oh my God. Kayla!" Violet rushed over to her friend and knelt on the cool tile floor in front of the tub.

Kayla was slumped over in the bathtub, holding both hands over her abdomen. Her emerald green dress was torn and blood dripped down the bottom of the bathtub, staining the pristine white surface red.

"What happened? Did Jess find out what we were doing? What does he know?" Violet rapid fired the questions, contemplating what she should do. She tried her best to think clearly. She could worry about Jess later. First, she needed to see how badly Kayla was injured and try to stop the bleeding.

She rummaged around in the cabinet underneath the sink and found a towel. She pressed it to Kayla's side and held it against the wound. "What happened?" she asked again.

"Stop... him," Kayla whispered.

"What did he do?! Where is he?" Violet asked urgently.

"He stabbed me with... his knife. I tried to... stop..." Kayla's eyelids fluttered and remained closed.

"Kayla! Please. You can't close your eyes right now. You need to stay awake."

Violet knew she couldn't waste time trying to get answers out of Kayla. She needed to save her. She pulled her phone out of her purse and dialed 911, and explained the situation. She answered their questions and gave the dispatcher the address of the cabin, telling them to hurry, panic-stricken that it was already too late.

Violet gently shook her friend, willing her to open her eyes. "Wake up. You can't be unconscious. The 911 dispatcher told me to make sure you stay awake. You're going to be okay, I promise. An ambulance is on its way here." Violet sniffled as a few tears ran down her cheeks. She climbed into the bathtub and held the towel against Kayla's side as the blood continued to drip.

# Chapter 33:
# After Jess

*November 9, 2019*

Wailing sirens pierced through the party sounds, then shortly after, the sound of teenagers scrambling to sober up, hide the alcohol, and put clothes back on for the ones who were in various stages of undress. Panic invaded the air as everyone wondered what was going on. They probably thought someone had called the cops about the underage teenagers drinking in the woods. Violet could imagine how terrified some of her classmates were at the thought of being arrested. She needed to go downstairs to answer the door before someone else did.

"I'm going to talk to the dispatcher and bring them up here to check on you. I'll be right back, okay?"

Violet was unsure if Kayla nodded in response or if she imagined it, so she hurried out of the room, down the stairs, and to the front door. She opened the door and revealed a tall, thin man with an impressive mustache.

She introduced herself as the one who made the phone call. The ambulance dispatcher's name was John. He had a calming presence as he asked her questions about what happened. She led him to the upstairs bathroom where Kayla waited in the bathtub. John inspected Kayla and gently tried to wake her up.

Violet's anxiety flowed through her body like an electric shock. Kayla had to make it. She had to be all right. This wasn't part of their plan. This wasn't how it was supposed to go. And where the hell was Jess?

After Kayla had been lifted into the ambulance and her vitals were checked, John said, "Violet?" in a tone that implied he had said her name at least once already.

Violet forced herself to turn her attention back to John. "Yes?"

"I said, do you know what happened to your friend? Was it an accident? Were you kids maybe... I don't know... messing around with something dangerous?" John prodded.

"No! It wasn't an accident. I think I know who stabbed her, but I don't know where they are. They might have left the party already."

"Okay, then you'll need to stay here and tell the police what happened when they arrive."

"What? I want to go with Kayla to the hospital! She shouldn't be alone when she wakes up. She'll be terrified and confused," Violet pleaded.

Violet looked at Kayla's unconscious body lying on the gurney in the ambulance, and her stomach clenched. This was all her fault. If she hadn't dragged Kayla into her own plan, then this wouldn't have happened. Why had she thought they could cross Jess and get away with it? She had underestimated how far he would go.

"I think it's best if you stay here. You aren't family, are you? We rarely allow non-relatives in the ambulance. It's my job to make sure she gets to the hospital and hopefully she'll be all right. Come to the hospital after you've talked to the police." John smiled sympathetically and closed the ambulance doors. He gestured at the driver, who immediately turned the siren on and peeled out of the cabin's circular driveway.

"Wait!" Violet yelled, fruitlessly chasing after the ambulance.

Her mind whirled. Jess. She needed to find Jess.

A girl with ridiculously long red hair, wearing an ankle-length fuchsia silk dress and a matching mask, came up to her. Her mask only covered her eyes, so Violet could see the freckles that stood out across her white skin—it was Savannah. "Hey, what happened? Is Kayla going to be all right?"

"I don't know," Violet sobbed, no longer able to hold her emotions in check.

The redhead took off her mask and reached out to Violet hesitantly, as if she was going to pat her on the shoulder or hug her, but pulled her hand back as if she changed her mind. Savannah wasn't exactly the person she wanted to be talking to right now, but she was more alone than ever.

"Violet?" Savannah said when Violet didn't respond and continued blankly staring at her. "Are you okay?

She nodded numbly, trying to remember how to form coherent words. "Someone stabbed Kayla."

Savannah gasped and literally clutched at the pearls around her neck. She was the true embodiment of a stereotypical Southern belle. "Who?" She stepped closer to Violet, waiting for the gossip.

Violet shook her head, knowing she couldn't tell her the truth. Savannah was the biggest gossip at their high school. If she said it was Jess, then the entire school would know before the weekend was over. "I can't say. The police are going to be here soon," she whispered.

"Was it Jess?" Savannah's eyes gleamed with interest. Apparently, she wouldn't give up.

"I don't want to talk about it."

"Okay, understandable. I hope Kayla's all right. Let me know if you need someone to talk to." Savannah grabbed Violet's phone from where it stuck out of her purse, prompted her to unlock it, and added herself as a new contact. "There. Now you have my phone number. Just text me if you want to talk!" Savannah waved and trotted away, her metallic silver heels clicking with every step on the pavement.

When Violet didn't think things could get any weirder, Jess came running up to her with his eyebrows scrunched together in worry. His brown curls were messier than usual, and he wasn't wearing a masquerade mask.

Jess pulled her into a tight hug without saying a word, then held her at arm's length, searching her eyes. "Where have you been? What happened? Where's Kayla?"

By this point, Violet was sure she was in an alternate universe. Surely, he was only pretending he wasn't aware of what was going on. Based on what Kayla had tried to tell her and what she assumed Jess's reaction would have been to stop their plan, he was the only one who could have stabbed Kayla. Now wasn't the time to second guess herself, but she was much too tired to put up a fight.

Violet wobbled as her legs gave out, but Jess was close enough and still holding onto her arms, so he caught her before she could fall. She let herself melt into his arms, relishing the embrace of her boyfriend. The one who had tried to kill her closest friend.

***

When the police arrived, they asked to question Violet, Jess, and any other witnesses who might have seen what happened to Kayla separately. For a moment, Violet debated what she should tell them. Should she lie? Should she pretend she didn't know Jess had been the one to stab Kayla? Or should she reveal everything she knew? Maybe she could fix this issue if she was careful. She might be able to solve a few of their problems. If only she had gotten more information from Kayla before the ambulance took her to the hospital. Then maybe she could make the right decision.

"Ms. Hale, your brave actions might have saved the life of your friend. Good job calling 911 so quickly and not freezing in a tense situation. You did the right thing," one of the police officers, a short, stocky middle-aged man, told her.

The other police officer, who was a young man with a buzz-cut who barely looked older than Violet, stared at her quizzically. "Do you know who did this to your friend? You mentioned you weren't around when it happened, but you were the one who found her?"

Violet swallowed nervously and sweat trickled down her back, despite the chilly temperature in the mountains. "Yes, I think I know who did it."

"You *think* you know?" the middle-aged police officer asked.

Violet rubbed her arms in a vain attempt to warm herself up. A strapless dress had been a terrible idea. "It was Mallory. Mallory McKenzie stabbed Kayla."

# Chapter 34: After Jess

*November 10, 2019*

Violet convinced the police officers she was fine driving herself home. She disabled the security alarm at her house and unlocked the front door. She heard someone moving in the family room and her dad stepped into the hall.

"Dad?" Violet said, questioning why he was downstairs during this time of night. He was wearing sweatpants and a T-shirt and his short hair stood up, as if he had been sleeping. "Why are you still up?"

Her dad blinked blearily and rubbed his hand through his hair. He ignored her question. "Violet? What are you doing home? I thought you were staying the night at your friend's house."

Violet shook her head and as she attempted to tell him what had happened, a sob escaped her mouth. Her dad looked at her with alarm. It had been a long time since he had seen her cry.

"Honey, are you okay? What's wrong?"

Tears rushed frantically down her cheeks. Her dad lurched forward and wrapped her into a bear hug, the most comforting hug she had felt in weeks.

"It will be okay, I promise. Everything's going to be okay," her dad attempted to soothe her. She wanted to believe him, but he didn't have a clue what she was dealing with.

She desperately wanted to tell him everything and let him fix it, like he had always done when she was young. He used to be the one she turned to for everything as a kid. A scraped knee from falling while rollerblading. A bad grade on a spelling test. A book recommendation when she couldn't decide what to read. But she didn't think even her dad could help her out of this one.

"Kayla was stabbed," she blurted out, deciding she could at least tell him the worst of what had happened. She needed someone to talk to, and her dad was the best option at the moment.

"What? Is she okay? How did this happen?" he asked, his eyes weary.

"We were at a party—"

Her dad eyed her dress. "Well, I figured that," he said with a small smile.

"Mallory stabbed her," Violet managed to say through her uncontrollable crying.

Her dad's eyes widened even more, but this time in shock. "Mallory? The one who—"

"Yeah." Violet sniffled as she tried to regain her composure.

"Where's Kayla? Is she at the hospital? We need to tell the police what happened." Her dad let go of her and rushed around frantically, most likely looking for his cellphone.

"Dad, I already talked to the police. Kayla's at the hospital. They wouldn't let me visit her because I'm not family, but I'll contact her mom tomorrow and ask for an update." Violet wandered into the family room and sank onto the sectional couch, barely noticing the pillow and quilt on the couch.

Her dad rubbed his eyes and looked at her. "Okay." He nodded slowly. "We'll go to the hospital tomorrow to see Kayla. I'll drive you." As he noticed Violet was about to protest and remind him that she had her driver's license and her own car now that she was sixteen, he said, "You aren't going there by yourself. No one should have to deal with something like this alone. I won't let you feel alone."

Violet smiled, despite her mounting anxiety, worry about whether Kayla would be okay, fear that she had lied to the police and her dad—and she honestly wasn't sure which lie was more terrifying—and panic over trying to stay away from Jess without Kayla around to act as a buffer and make sure she didn't have to be alone with him. Never mind the fact that she was potentially dating a murderer. "Thanks."

"You should go to bed. Get some sleep."

"Okay. Night."

"Goodnight. See you in the morning." Her dad returned to his spot on the couch.

Violet walked up the stairs to her bedroom without mentioning to her dad that she had noticed the quilt and pillow on the couch or asking him again why he had obviously been sleeping downstairs. She had enough to worry about without wondering whether her parents' fighting had worsened and their marriage was disintegrating. She didn't want to be selfish, but she would talk to her dad more in the morning and make sure he was fine. Her parents wouldn't get divorced. It was a rough patch, probably. Every relationship went through those.

She removed her makeup from her face, hung her dress in her closet, and put on her softest, ugliest sweatpants and a sweater that was much too big, but comforting. She brushed her teeth and finally crawled into bed, glancing at the time on her phone. 2 a.m. She hoped she could fall asleep. She needed to rest if she wanted to be at the top of her game tomorrow. And she needed to be if she wanted to get out of this mess alive.

***

*November 10, 2019*

When Violet woke up and prepared for the day, she entered the kitchen to find an elaborate breakfast spread across the counter. Her dad stood in front of the electric skillet, flipping a chocolate chip pancake, then adding it to a stack towering on a plate on the counter.

"Good morning," he greeted her with a grin.

"Morning. What's all this?" She couldn't remember the last time her dad cooked breakfast like this. Usually, he told Violet and her siblings to grab a bowl of cereal or a banana, even on the weekends. And she couldn't remember an instance of her mom cooking, except maybe Kraft mac and cheese a handful of times. Her dad was the one who always made sure they had something to eat.

"Breakfast," her dad said with a chuckle.

Violet rolled her eyes good-naturedly. "I meant why?"

He shrugged. "Breakfast is the most important meal of the day. I'll drive you to the hospital after we eat."

While Violet ate her third pancake, Emilia and Glenn stumbled into the kitchen, just as surprised to see a full breakfast prepared for them. They caught up on what was going on in each of their lives, with Violet glossing over the details of the masquerade party. She wanted to keep the conversation light and not ruin everyone's day. Violet assumed her mom was still sleeping, staying in bed until late morning like she usually did on weekends. It was just as well; she probably would have ruined their family time, anyway.

Her dad stood from the table when he had finished eating and washed the dishes, while addressing his other two kids. "I'm going to take Violet to the hospital to visit Kayla. I'm not sure how long we'll be gone, but we're ordering pizza for dinner and having a family game night tonight."

"But Dad, I was going to go to Macy's house tonight!" Emilia protested.

"Call her and cancel. We need to spend more time together as a family," their dad said sternly.

"I was going to play video games tonight!" Glenn complained.

Violet laughed sarcastically. "Really? That's your excuse?"

Emilia giggled too. "Ugh, fine. I'll tell her I can't come over. But I won't call her. I'll text her like a normal person."

"Good. Dinner is at 6 p.m., then games. It will be fun!" their dad promised.

Emilia and Glenn scampered off to their respective bedrooms. Violet followed her dad outside to his car and he drove her to the hospital.

When they arrived, her dad turned to her, his hands gripping the steering wheel. They hadn't talked much on the drive over, except her dad asking if she had any particular games she wanted to play and making sure that her favorite type of pizza was still sausage with extra cheese.

"I know there's something you're not telling me about the party last night. I'm not sure why you don't think you can be honest with me. Maybe I haven't been around enough and you don't trust me anymore." He relaxed his grip and dropped his hands from the steering wheel. "I've tried to be a good dad to you, Emilia, and Glenn, but I'm not perfect, and I come up short sometimes. I try to make up for your mom—" He cleared his throat, realizing he had said too much. "Anyway, I want the best for you and your siblings, and I want you to know I'm here for you no matter what, Violet. And if you want to tell me the truth about the party, you can. Understand?"

"Okay. Thanks. And you haven't failed, despite what you may think. You make up for mom's shortcomings." Violet smiled at him and opened the passenger door of the car, stepping outside.

Her dad followed her into the hospital. They reached the front desk and spoke to the woman working.

"We're here to see a patient who was admitted last night. Kayla Stewart," her dad explained to the administrative worker.

The woman eyed them suspiciously. "Are you relatives of the patient you wish to visit?"

"No, my daughter is friends with her."

The woman smiled grimly. "I'm afraid you won't be able to see her then."

Violet's face fell. She wondered if Kayla's mom had visited her yet. She didn't want Kayla to wake up by herself. She didn't know if she would remember everything that happened, but she wanted to make sure she was all right. "Can you at least tell me how she is? Please?" Violet begged.

The woman sighed and typed something on her computer. "Kayla Stewart, you said?"

Violet nodded vigorously, hoping the woman would change her mind.

The woman squinted at her computer, clicked a few things, then something printed from the printer next to her computer. She handed them each a visitor's badge. "Here. She's in Room 311. You can take the elevator or the stairs."

Violet's dad smiled gratefully. "We appreciate it. Have a good day!"

Violet's dad put his hand on her back and guided her to the elevator. Thankfully, they were the only two people in the elevator, because Violet didn't think she could handle anything else occurring before they saw Kayla. They exited the elevator and followed the numbers on the doors as they climbed higher. They stopped in front of Room 311.

"I'll let you talk to her. Tell her we're all thinking about her." Her dad stopped outside the room. "I'm going to find some coffee."

"Okay."

Violet knocked on the door as her dad walked away.

"Come in," a voice called from inside the room.

Violet opened the door. Kayla was lying in a hospital bed, wearing one of those flimsy papery gowns, hooked up to IVs. Her purple hair fell lank and lifeless around her face and she had bags under her eyes, suggesting she hadn't slept well. Despite all this, she smiled brightly when she saw Violet.

"Hey."

"Are you okay?" Violet rushed over to Kayla and hovered by the bed.

"The doctors said I'm lucky you found me when you did. If you had waited to call 911 or if no one had found me—" Kayla shuddered. Violet assumed they were thinking similar things about what could have happened. Things could have ended so differently. So much worse.

Violet pulled up a chair and sat beside Kayla's bed. "Sorry to bring this up again. I'm sure you don't want to relive all the gory details, but what exactly happened last night? You were trying to tell me something, but you fell unconscious and I wasn't able to get much out of you."

Kayla attempted to sit up straighter and winced from the pain in her abdomen, clutching it as if it would help ease the pain. She breathed slowly and laid back down. "When I was inside the kitchen switching out the drinks that Jess planned on using to poison everyone, he caught me. He wasn't supposed to be there yet, but he was. And Violet... I have to tell you something else."

"I figured he caught you. What else happened?"

"He forced me to follow him to one of the spare bedrooms. He claimed it was so we could talk alone without being overheard, but I assumed he would try to hurt me. When he wasn't looking, I grabbed a knife in the kitchen, then I followed him upstairs. He opened the door to a bedroom, and he instantly started fighting with me."

"So, Jess really stabbed you?" Violet asked, astounded, even though it was what she had suspected.

Kayla's face seemed to pale even more. "Yeah. He wouldn't listen to me. I tried reasoning with him and telling him that he couldn't resort to murder. That he was worse than the popular kids if he killed them instead of facing them and dealing with his issues. He noticed I had a knife and became furious. He asked if I was scared of him, then he grabbed the knife from me and I lunged for him. I don't know if he actually meant to hurt me so badly… I would like to believe that he still cares about me." Kayla's face reflected the disappointment in their supposed friend.

Violet shook her head in disbelief at what had happened. "I think he cares about you. In his own sick and twisted way."

"I thought so too until last night. Violet, even if he didn't mean to seriously injure me, he left me lying on the floor bleeding. He left me to die. He could have called 911 or tried to get help, but he didn't. I must have crawled to the bathroom and passed out from the pain. The next thing I knew, I woke up in the bathtub with you there," Kayla explained quietly.

"I'm sorry about what happened, and that I wasn't with you to stop him. But don't worry, I have a plan," Violet said, as the plan formed in her mind. "I already told my dad and the police that Mallory was the one who stabbed you."

"Um, why did you do that? You know it was Jess," Kayla retorted, scratching her head.

"Jess is the only who knows what really happened besides you. Who are the police going to believe? The popular girl who terrorizes everyone? The boy who has anger issues and convinced us to kill Jimmy? Or the victim who was stabbed? We can tell the police everything. If we tell them that Jess convinced us that killing Jimmy was the right move and that he coerced us into staying quiet, and that Mallory stabbed you, then we can take down both of them. I think we'll get out of this."

Kayla bit her lip, quietly contemplating Violet's words. "I keep thinking this is all some twisted joke. Jess and I have been there for each other for everything since middle school. We were all each other had. I still can't believe he betrayed me. And I thought he was falling in love with you. I would have warned you if I thought he would do something like this to you. Or maybe, somehow, he thinks this is what you do for the people you love? Was he just using me this whole time to help him get what he wanted? I never imagined—"

"It's not your fault. He had us all fooled." Violet's face set into a grim expression as she pondered everything she had just learned. "We're going to change the rest of the plan. Jess proved he isn't friends with us and he doesn't care about either of us. He convinced us to kill Jimmy. He tried to force us to poison nearly a hundred of our classmates. He stabbed you and left you to die." Violet paused, steadying her uneven breathing as she revealed her new plan to Kayla. "I have a new deep, dark desire. I want to make sure Jess goes to prison."

# Chapter 35:
# After Jess

*November 13, 2019*

Three days later, Kayla's doctor discharged her from the hospital. The doctor told her to take it easy for a while. Violet checked on her every day. As each day passed that week, they perfected their plan. It was time for them to stop Jess once and for all. He was evil, sadistic, and had planned on killing multiple people. Wasn't it better if they got rid of him? The longer he lived, surely the more damage he could cause, especially now that he had harmed Kayla. How long would it be until he tried to hurt Violet too?

On Monday, Jess walked into school with a crazed look in his eyes.

"What's wrong?" Violet asked, already in a panic as a dozen scenarios flew through her mind. What had he done now? And what would it take to stop him?

"Mallory…" was all he uttered as he threw himself into her arms and held her. "I think she's dead," he said softly, nuzzling his head into her shoulder.

Violet froze; her body posture stiffened as Jess gripped her closely. She couldn't form coherent thoughts. She could barely register the other students walking by them in the hall.

"What happened?" she finally choked out.

Jess pulled his face away from her shoulder and stared into her eyes. "The poison at the party." An evil grin spread across his face, and an icy feeling washed over Violet. "It worked."

"What? But I thought—"

"That Kayla stopped me?" Jess shook his head slowly, as if she had disappointed him. "I decided she was right. At least, partially. There was no need to kill everyone at the party. Just Mallory. So, I did."

"What did you do?" Violet hissed.

Jess shrugged and placed his hands on Violet's shoulders. "I only did what you wanted. I made sure she was the only one whose drink was spiked. I promise I didn't hurt anyone else." His green eyes were wide and innocent. "I did it for you. Now we can be together without Mallory interfering. She can't ruin your life anymore."

"Jess, this isn't—I didn't want—"

"Don't you dare tell me you didn't want her dead! Or have you been lying to me this whole time?" Now his eyes blazed with a fire that Violet wasn't sure she could put out.

She did her best to soften her voice. She could pretend for a while longer. "No, you're right. I would never lie to you." She wrapped her arms around him and embraced him, trying not to tremble as he returned the hug.

Violet had enough of being bullied, used, and taken advantage of. She was no longer the timid, insecure girl everyone thought she was. She wouldn't let anyone walk all over her ever again, not even Jess. She wasn't the quiet girl anymore. And she would make sure everyone knew.

***

The school day seemed to drag by slowly, just like the days before she met Jess. Kayla wouldn't be back at school until next week. Violet planned to bring Kayla her homework after school, so she wouldn't get too behind while she was at home healing.

During her lunch period, Violet briefly contemplated going to the library to hide. She didn't want to run into Jess or any of Mallory's friends, since they all shared the same lunch period. But at the last minute, she turned around and headed to the cafeteria. She deserved to eat her lunch in peace. She shouldn't have to hide.

While she waited in line, someone tapped on her shoulder and she whirled around, anxiety rushing through her veins like a jolt of caffeine. Despite what she had tried to convince herself for the past twenty-four hours since she learned about Jess's betrayal, the second she stared into his green eyes, her heart stuttered with emotion. Of course she still cared about him; that wouldn't vanish in one day. She was naïve to think she could ignore how much she cared, despite everything he had done. She felt at war with herself, battling a multitude of emotions.

"Hey," he said.

She turned around to face the front of the line again, not bothering to respond. She wasn't sure she could handle this right now. Her emotions weren't in check, and she struggled to stay calm. A war had been raging inside of her since earlier in the day when Jess had revealed that he thought he had killed Mallory.

"Violet." He smiled, stepping forward so he was next to her in the line. He grabbed her hand.

"What do you want?" She gritted her teeth and yanked her hand away from his.

"Why are you upset with me? I thought you understood what I did—" Jess started, rubbing the back of his neck.

"Well, you were wrong."

"Uh, okay. I'm sorry for—"

Violet laughed harshly as her mask slipped. "Which part are you referring to? Stabbing Kayla?" Her face burned as other students in the line stared at them and eavesdropped on their conversation. Most people had already heard what happened to Kayla and Mallory, and many of them probably assumed that she and Jess were involved.

Jess frowned and touched her shoulder, but Violet jerked away from him.

"Don't you dare touch me."

"You don't understand what happ—"

"You're right, and I don't think you can make me understand your actions, so don't bother trying."

"How's Kayla doing?" he asked quietly, changing the subject.

"You don't have the right to know anything about Kayla after what you did to her. She trusted you, and so did I," Violet responded, her eyes glinting with anger.

"Okay, but I wanted to apologize. Can you please just tell Kayla—"

"Get away from her, you douche!" a random person in line near them shouted.

"Yeah, leave her alone, Jess! She's too good for you," someone else chimed in.

Jess's face reddened, and he exited the line, weaving in and out of the throngs of students to make his way out of the cafeteria.

Violet smiled triumphantly. She may not have won the battle yet, but at least people seemed to be on her side. For once, her classmates sided with her. Too bad it had taken something so horrible occurring for people to root for her.

Violet grabbed her lunch tray, which was piled high with food, and found an empty table. She pulled out a book from her backpack, set it on the table, and took out the bookmark holding her page. One thing hadn't changed in her life. Books were her escape, her comfort when everything went wrong. But this time felt different. She had stood up to Jess. She hadn't bent to his will and accepted his apology. She had spoken up. She was proud of herself for staying strong, and she thought Kayla would be too.

***

Later that afternoon, Violet sat on a worn armchair in Kayla's basement/makeshift bedroom, while Kayla sat in her bed, propped up with a mountain of pillows behind her. Violet had brought over a pizza. She wasn't sure how well Kayla's mom was doing after

Jimmy's death and her daughter's near-death experience so soon after. She didn't know if Kayla's mom had been cooking lately or taking care of her. It turned out she hadn't been feeling up to much of anything, so Kayla was grateful for the pizza. She had been living off takeout food whenever her mom remembered they needed to eat.

Violet finished telling Kayla what had happened that day at school and what Jess said to her.

"Wow. He has balls to think he could apologize to you for stabbing me and that you would be fine with it. I wonder what he was trying to accomplish?" Kayla contemplated, while grabbing another slice of thin crust sausage pizza.

"Who knows? He's clearly delusional."

"I'm proud of you for not going along with it, though. That took a lot of courage," Kayla said with a smile. "And when I'm back at school, I hope he's smart enough to not try talking to me. I'll knock his lights out."

Violet returned Kayla's smile. "Thanks. I know you will."

"You know what I'm still confused about?"

"Hmm?" Violet asked with a mouthful of pizza.

"Why did Jess change the plan at the last minute and only poison Mallory? And why did he stab me if he knew I was right? Plus, why haven't the police brought any of us in for questioning, especially if Mallory is dead? Why is no one talking about it?" Kayla chewed her pizza slowly as she tried to piece it all together.

Violet pondered Kayla's questions for a minute. "You're right. It doesn't add up, but I'm sure there's an explanation. I think we need to talk to one of Mallory's friends and get their insight into the situation.

I bet Savannah will tell us. If she knows anything, she's sure to spill it. Maybe she saw something at the party."

"True, that girl needs to learn to keep her mouth shut. But we can use it to our advantage."

Violet nodded and wiped her greasy hands on a paper towel. "That's our next move. I'll talk to Savannah at school tomorrow and try to convince her to tell me what she knows about that night. Something is off about this whole thing, and I'm going to figure out what it is."

Kayla frowned. "I feel so sick about it all. Mallory was awful to you, but it shouldn't have turned out this way."

"I know. I didn't really want her to die. I can't believe Jess followed through with it."

"It was always just... something we talked about. I know Jess had his whole elaborate, multi-step plan, but I thought it was one of those fantasies, something you imagine doing, but would never act on. I didn't think it was a legitimate plan. He became obsessed, though. I don't know what changed." Kayla paused as she began to sob. "It was different with Jimmy. You understand, right? You know what he did to my mom and I. I *hated* Jimmy; he was one of the most awful people I've ever met. I wanted him away from my mom and me, so he couldn't hurt us anymore... Is it so wrong that I wanted him dead? But Jess is taking it too far. His quest for revenge is consuming him. I never thought we would kill Mallory or half the students in our grade. I don't want to be a murderer! After Jimmy—"

"It's not your fault, Kayla. You tried to stop him and look what happened to you." Violet gestured to Kayla's abdomen, which was still covered in a heavy bandage. "You did everything you could."

# Chapter 36:
# After Jess

*November 14, 2019*

Savannah tossed her red hair over her shoulder and smiled at Violet, glancing around the hall as she did so. "Let's go somewhere a little quieter." She grabbed hold of Violet's arm, linking their arms together and tugging her into a room that turned out to be a utility closet.

Violet swallowed nervously as Savannah shut the door behind them.

"Now, what did you want to talk about?" Savannah arched one perfectly manicured eyebrow.

Violet breathed deeply. Kayla was counting on her. She needed to keep her resolve. "What do you know about Mallory's birthday party?"

Savannah enveloped her in a smothering hug. "Oh, honey! I was so sorry to hear about your break-up with Jess. I thought you two were the cutest."

"Uh—" Violet replied brilliantly, trying to extricate herself from Savannah's embrace in the tight space. "We didn't break up."

"Hmm, that's not what I heard. So, from what Mallory told me, Jess texted her before Halloween. He was all pouty and sad that you wouldn't have sex with him, which, like, I totally respect that you wanted to wait. But Mallory saw it as her chance to get him back. She wanted to sink her claws into him again." Savannah paused and tapped her finger on her perfectly glossed lips. "He told her to back off, though. He told her he made a mistake in texting her and she was *pissed.*"

Violet couldn't help but feel a twinge of happiness at the fact that Jess had chosen her over Mallory. She needed to remind herself of all the terrible things he had done. She knew he wasn't good for her, even if he truly cared for her, albeit in a sick and twisted way.

"You were involved in planning Mallory's birthday party, right?" Violet prompted, trying to steer the conversation back to get the information she wanted.

"Oh, of course! I had been helping her plan it for months. We set everything up for it to be the perfect sixteenth birthday party." Savannah's delicate face darkened and tears seemed to come out of nowhere. "I never expected... what happened."

"I've only heard rumors. What happened that night?" Violet lied.

"Mallory told Tanner to meet her in an upstairs bedroom in the cabin, then she went downstairs to get drinks. I think they were planning to, you know—but she never made it back upstairs." More tears fell from Savannah's eyes and splashed onto her crisp pink shirt.

"I'm sorry, Savannah." Violet realized she needed to comfort her if she didn't want to seem like a complete bitch. Besides, she felt bad for her. Savannah hadn't been the one to torture her. She hadn't stopped Mallory, but she had tried to intervene a few times. She was clearly more caring than Mallory was.

Savannah swiped a tear from her eye; her eyes glistened with fresh tears as she stared at Violet. "I just hope she's going to make it. Sure, Mallory could be a bitch, but I didn't want her to die!"

"Wait. What?"

Savannah bit her lip so hard that she smudged some of her sparkly lip gloss. "Promise you won't tell anyone. I swear, I didn't mean to kill her. I just wanted to—to freak her out."

Violet tilted her head. This was an interesting turn of events. "I won't tell anyone. I just need to know everything that happened that night."

"Why do you want to know? What are you going to do?" Savannah twirled her red hair around her fingers.

Violet dug her heels in. This was it. "I'm going to get revenge, of course. What else?"

Savannah smiled sadly. "I didn't think you had it in you."

"People aren't always what they appear to be," Violet said.

"True. I'm still mad at Mallory for what she did to me over the summer."

Now Violet was curious about what Savannah had referred to. "What did Mallory do to you? I thought you were best friends."

"We are, but... it's complicated being friends with her. Please don't tell anyone, but I've had a crush on Izzy forever, and I think she's just *the cutest*. She's so sweet and loves animals. Someday, she wants to be a vet. Izzy is the best person I know. I was going to tell her how I feel at Mallory's birthday party, but when Mallory found out, she set Izzy up with some guy on the basketball team. She thought if Izzy and I started dating, then it would ruin the vibe of our group or something. And never mind her not wanting me to make a big deal out of it and, like, ruin her birthday." Savannah rolled her eyes. "As if she's the only one who's allowed to find love."

"That's bullshit," Violet said. "I think you should tell Izzy how you feel and see if she feels the same way. It would be worth the risk if she likes you too."

"I don't know. She has a boyfriend now and I think she really likes him. Besides, I'm not sure she feels the same about me." Savannah sighed, looking unsure of herself. It threw Violet off because she saw Savannah as the ultra-confident, charismatic, popular person.

"You won't know unless you give it a shot. It could be something great."

"Maybe you're right. Did you know Mallory knew about her dad and Izzy's mom hooking up for months? Apparently, Mallory caught them in the act and her dad paid her off to make her stay quiet about it. She hid it from Izzy. It makes me so mad that she would hide something like that from one of her friends," Savannah babbled on when Violet said nothing. "She has dirt on all of us, and I honestly think that's why everyone is still friends with her. They're all too scared to stand up to her. They think if they take a stand against her, then she'll tell everyone their deepest, darkest secrets. And knowing Mallory, she probably would. I had to take circumstances into my own hands!"

"It didn't go how you planned, though?" Violet prompted.

Savannah shook her head. She had stopped crying and seemed to be calmer now. "I poured some laxatives into her drink. I don't know if it was because it was combined with alcohol, or what, but apparently it really fucked her up."

Violet chewed her lip thoughtfully. "What if there was something else in the drink? Like... poison?"

Savannah gasped and held her hand over her mouth, muffling her response slightly. "I swear I didn't poison her! I would never do something so awful. I just wanted to embarrass her and ruin her night. I thought it would be terrible for her reputation if she had to spend all night in the bathroom. I planned to tell everyone what was going on."

"It was Jess," Violet said in a barely audible voice. "He thought he was getting even for me. He took things too far." Violet paused as she recalled what Savannah had said a few minutes ago. "So, is Mallory—"

"She's expected to make a full recovery. She's already trying to convince the doctors to let her leave the hospital so she can go to the fall ball. She's incredibly lucky that she didn't ingest more of that drink. Tanner, on the other hand—"

"Tanner's in the hospital too?" This was news to Violet. All everyone had been talking about was Mallory.

"Yeah, he's in much worse shape than Mallory. If what you said is true and Jess poisoned her drink, maybe it was in Tanner's drink too? Or maybe they shared a drink that night?"

"I think you're on to something. Savannah, how would you like to join me and Kayla in our plan?"

"And what kind of plan would that be?" Savannah asked in her southern accent, with a hand on her hip.

"A plan for revenge. A plan to get back at Mallory and Jess for everything they've done to all of us. A plan to make things even for all their betrayals."

Savannah bit her lip. "I don't know. I already feel guilty about what happened to Mallory, and I don't really have a reason to want revenge on Jess—"

Violet cut in. "That's where you're wrong. The incident at Mallory's party might have shaken her up a little, but I bet in a few weeks, she'll be right back to acting how she was before. It won't stop her from bullying people, including her friends. Don't you want to tell Izzy how you feel and have a chance to be with her? I don't think that's possible as long as Mallory is intent on keeping her from you. Plus, you said Mallory knew about her dad's affair with Izzy's mom and didn't tell Izzy. What type of person keeps such a horrible thing from their friend? And as far as Jess goes, the breakup with Mallory messed him up. He won't stop until he gets revenge on everyone he thinks wronged him. His original plan was to poison everyone at Mallory's birthday party and that would have included you, so—"

A sinister smile curled up Savannah's pretty face. "I'm in." She held out her hand for Violet to shake.

Violet shook her hand and gave a sinister smile of her own. "I think it's going to be a pleasure working with you."

***

*November 14, 2019*

Kayla handed her a bag of BBQ chips, and Violet grabbed a handful. "So, Savannah's on our side now?"

"It appears so."

"I'm not sure I trust someone who will turn that easily," Kayla said, squinting at Violet.

"Me neither, but we don't need to fully trust her, as long as she helps us and doesn't let Mallory or Jess know what we're scheming."

Kayla groaned dramatically. "Trusting Savannah to be quiet about a crazy secret and not tell anyone? Yeah, like that's going to end well."

"It's the best option we have. Besides, Savannah feels like Mallory betrayed her and Izzy, so I think she'll stay quiet this time. She did put laxatives in her drink."

Kayla giggled. "I can't believe she did that. But let's hope so. It would be helpful having an insider from Mallory's cult on our side."

"Exactly. It gives us an advantage. Mallory will have no clue what hit her," Violet said with a grin.

"You sound like an evil villain."

"Maybe I am now. It sounds more fun than my former identity as the quiet, book nerd."

"Hey, I never thought you were a nerd. I mean, maybe I did… but in the best way possible. Not in a mean way," Kayla quickly amended her statement.

"Uh, thanks?" Violet snatched the chip bag away from Kayla. "I'll be glad when you're back at school. It's a nightmare fielding everyone's questions and dealing with all the stares and gossip by myself."

"I bet. I'm sorry you're dealing with all that. Have you seen Jess again?"

"Thankfully, I haven't. I never want to look at his cute, stupid face again."

"Yeah, me neither," Kayla agreed. "Thanks for coming over again. It's boring sitting in bed all day. I think I miss being around people and I never thought that would happen!"

Violet laughed. "Tomorrow's Friday, so you just have to make it through the weekend. Then you'll be back at school on Monday, right?"

"Yup, the doctor said it's fine as long as I continue resting this weekend. I'm feeling much better than I was a few days ago. Vicodin is a wonderful thing."

"Good, I'm glad you're doing better. I was so worried about you. Do you want to sleep over at my house tomorrow?"

"If my mom will let me," Kayla muttered.

"Seriously? I thought your mom didn't care what you did."

"Yeah, that was before her boyfriend committed suicide and I got stabbed by my supposed best friend. Now she's all paranoid that something's going to happen to me. She's been smothering me all week. I'll be ecstatic when I'm back at school and can escape her during the day," Kayla complained.

"Okay, then I think a sleepover is definitely necessary. We both need a fun, normal night of hanging out, eating junk food, and watching horror movies."

"And plotting how to get revenge on our former best friend and his skank of an ex-girlfriend?" Kayla asked hopefully.

"Well, obviously. That was implied."

The Quiet Girl

# Chapter 37:
# After Jess

*November 15, 2019*

On Friday night, Violet and Kayla binge-watched horror movies, ate burritos from a new Mexican restaurant in downtown Asheville, and plotted revenge. Just a typical Friday night for normal teenage girls. They wanted to talk to Savannah the next day to figure out the details of the plan because she was an essential part of making sure their plan succeeded. They needed her to keep an eye on Jess and update them on anything that could help take him down.

The basic premise of their plan was to incapacitate him at the fall ball, which was one day away. Originally, Violet had thought she would go to the ball with Jess as her date, but clearly that was no longer the case. Instead, she and Kayla were going together, and the night wouldn't be anything like she had planned.

"Tell me again why our school has a fall ball, even though homecoming wasn't that long ago?"

"Who knows? I wouldn't even be going to this stupid thing if it wasn't for our plan. I hate school dances," Kayla complained. "Our school has a ridiculous number of dances. The town is obsessed with festivals and events to celebrate anything and everything, and it seems like everyone here is always looking for a new excuse to dress up in expensive clothes, dance, and get drunk. Although since this is a school event, it may be difficult to drink this time, especially since Jess used to raid his parent's stash for us."

"Drinking is the least of our concerns right now. We can worry about that later. What are we going to do at the ball to get back at Jess? We need to show him that we won't sit back and let him get away with everything." Violet paced her bedroom as she thought about the options. "It has to be something that will go undetected, something that can't be traced back to us, so we don't get in trouble."

"Right. Let me think for a minute. We'll come up with something."

"You're the one who's always watching horror movies! You should be bursting with revenge plots," Violet joked.

"Hmm. You have a point," Kayla responded seriously as she gazed out the window, deep in thought.

"But the real question is, how far do we take it? Do we scare him enough that he backs off? Or do we... take it further?"

Kayla stared at Violet uneasily, as if she was second guessing their idea. "I know Jess hurt both of us, but I don't think I can kill him. It was different with Jimmy."

"Jess tried to kill you! Doesn't that make you angry? Don't you want him to feel as scared and helpless as you did? Just imagine his face when he thinks he's going to die. It'll be priceless. I thought we were on the same page. You aren't backing out now, are you?" Violet moved closer to Kayla, closing in on her.

Kayla shrank away. "I just don't know if this is the answer. You already lied to the police about the details of what happened. In fact, I bet the police will bring Mallory and Jess both in for questioning if they haven't already. But Jess's parents are so wealthy, he'll probably get away with it without any consequences. They can afford to pay off whoever they want to."

"Exactly! That's why we have to stop him. The police won't do anything and neither will anyone else. It's up to us."

Kayla sighed loudly and set her half-finished burrito back in the takeout container, as if she was no longer hungry. "Okay, you're right. Let's come up with a solid plan, then."

***

*November 16, 2019*

On Saturday morning, they messaged Savannah and explained their plan. They decided it was easier to keep their communication over an encrypted messaging app on their phones. It was too risky to meet in person. Someone could see them together and question why Savannah was with Violet and Kayla. The app ensured no one could read their messages.

William cooked breakfast for Violet, her siblings, and Kayla. As usual, Jocelyn was nowhere to be found. Violet and Kayla hung out all day, so they could get ready together for the ball, then attend the event together. It was still mid-morning after they finished breakfast, so they went back upstairs to Violet's room to get dressed. Violet threw on a pair of jeans and a long-sleeved T-shirt, then brushed her hair, deciding she would worry more about her appearance later, when it was closer to the start time for the ball.

Jess had texted her and asked if they could still go together, like they had originally planned last month. Kayla told her to say she would meet Jess at the dance, which made sense, considering they hadn't technically broken up. Although she and Jess had barely spoken in days, Violet agreed. It would make their plan easier if she knew where Jess was and what he was up to during the ball, even if their relationship was over in Violet's mind. Jess must have thought he stood a chance of fixing things between them. Like it was something Violet could easily forgive—the equivalent of an argument over what to eat for dinner, instead of Jess trying to kill their friend...

While Violet had already been dressed and ready for several minutes, Kayla seemed to take a particularly long time to apply her eyeliner.

"Why are you putting on makeup right now? You'll probably have to fix it again before the ball."

Kayla's face turned a dark red. "It's not because of someone I like, if that's what you're thinking," she said defensively, nearly stabbing herself with her eyeliner pencil.

Violet burst out laughing. "Okay, that's not suspicious at all. It's totally because of a crush. Who is it?" She had never heard Kayla mention being attracted to anyone at school. Maybe whoever she liked went to a different school. But they weren't planning to go anywhere today, except for the ball later...

Kayla put down her eyeliner pencil and looked at Violet. "This is so awkward." She groaned and looked away. "I think your brother is cute."

"*Glenn?* Ew, oh God," Violet said in mock horror.

"I was planning to go downstairs and knock on his bedroom door to see if he wanted to hang out some time," Kayla mumbled as her cheeks blazed even more.

"He hasn't dated anyone in a while. I'm not sure how he'll react, but if he's going to date anyone, you're the type of girl he would go for."

"Uh, thanks?" Kayla brushed her purple hair and flicked it off her shoulders. "Okay, I'm going to talk to him."

Violet remained in her room, scrolling idly through Netflix as she waited for Kayla to return with news about her conquest or defeat. When her bedroom doorknob turned, she practically jumped out of bed to close the door behind Kayla.

Kayla had a huge grin on her face. "Glenn said yes. He thinks I'm pretty. He was so nervous and kept stuttering, so it made me feel less awkward." She laughed, her confidence back again.

"Aww. I mean, it's gross that you like my brother, but I would rather have you date him than some random girl. At least we're friends already."

"It's just one date, Violet. I don't even know if this will turn into anything. After the days I spent living here and getting to know him, I didn't want to miss out on something potentially great."

Violet thought back to when Kayla had lived with them. She hadn't thought much of it at the time, but Glenn seemed to come out of his room and hang out with the family more or found an excuse to be in the kitchen when Kayla was over. It made sense now.

"Well, I had no idea you two were interested in each other, but I'm happy for you," Violet said with a smile.

They hung out for the rest of the day and tried to enjoy their last day of being normal sixteen-year-old girls. Violet and Kayla were anything but normal, but they both had become pretty good at faking it.

# Chapter 38: After Jess

*November 16, 2019*

This was it—the moment Violet and Kayla had been waiting for—the night of the high school's annual fall ball. Not wanting to buy new outfits, they both wore the same dresses they had worn to Mallory's sixteenth birthday party. Violet hadn't worn hers since that night, so it was still in perfect condition. She fluffed out the tulle skirt and checked herself out in the bathroom mirror. Purple was her favorite color, and she loved the sequins on the dress. Luckily for Kayla, her mom, Molly, was an excellent seamstress and had somehow mended Kayla's dress where it had ripped after Jess stabbed her in the abdomen. She had even miraculously gotten the blood stain out.

Violet and Kayla strode into the high school's decorated gymnasium, keeping their eyes peeled for Jess. They had already texted Savannah to let her know they had arrived. Most of the students sat at the round tables. Despite the overly eager DJ's best attempts at playing school-appropriate and teenager-approved music, no one was dancing yet. The bass thumped obnoxiously throughout the room, making it difficult to hear anything else.

They found a table and set down their purses. Kayla went off to find soda, so Violet waited at the table by herself. Instead of pulling out her phone like most teenage girls would have, she gazed around the gymnasium, looking for Jess. Why did she want to see him? Morbid curiosity, maybe. She couldn't help it. It wasn't as if she hated him, though she had tried to convince herself she did. She found herself jumping back and forth from wanting him dead to caring about him, and then something in between. She didn't know how she would react when she saw him. But she didn't have to wait long to find out.

She finally spotted him across the room, looking as handsome as ever in a black suit with a purple bow tie that matched her dress; his brown curls tousled to perfection.

She met his gaze as he scanned the room. He smiled and quickly headed to her table. *Had he been looking for her too?* Her heart raced. Although she couldn't help herself from wondering why he had spent so much time with her, seemed so sweet, and almost had sex with her if he was planning on betraying her the whole time. Had he *really* never cared? And what about the fact that he stabbed Kayla, his best friend of nearly four years? None of it made any sense.

Kayla rejoined her at the table and set down two sodas. "Here, I know you like Mountain Dew."

"Thanks." Violet smiled.

"Have you seen Jess yet?"

"Yeah," she said bitterly and gestured, as Jess was nearly halfway to their table.

"Are you okay?"

"I'm fine. I just want to get this over with and go home."

"We don't have to follow through, you know. We can text Savannah and tell her to call it off. No one will be the wiser."

Violet shook her head. "No, we need to do it. I want him to pay."

Kayla popped the tab on her soda can and took a sip. "Okay, then let's do this."

Jess joined them at their table. Kayla turned to leave as soon as she made eye contact with Jess, but he grabbed her arm to stop her from walking away.

"Kayla, wait—please let me talk to you," Jess implored. His green eyes looked particularly innocent.

Kayla yanked her arm out of his grip and practically growled at Jess. "I don't want to talk to you. You betrayed me and a simple apology won't make up for that. You got all three of us into this mess." She snatched her purse from the table and slung it over her shoulder. "I'll see you later, Violet," she called as she walked away.

Violet waved goodbye to Kayla, then turned to face Jess. She didn't want to talk to him, but she had to. "Having fun?" she asked with a fake smile plastered on her face.

Jess tugged on his brown curls in frustration. "Not quite. I know I screwed up, so please just tell me how I can make it up to you."

"I can't do that. You're not—you're not good for me," she whispered, staring into his sparkling green eyes. She swore his eyes glistened with tears and she fought her emotions to not feel sorry for him.

Jess leaned forward and wrapped his arms around her, then buried his head into her shoulder. "Please, Violet. Please forgive me. I care about you."

Violet pretended to hug him back and swiped the silver lighter from his pocket while he was distracted, placed it in the pocket of her dress, and gently shoved him away.

"I can't do that. It's over, Jess."

\*\*\*

Violet received a text from Savannah.

**Savannah:** Ready!

**Violet:** Got it. I'm on the move.

Violet told Jess she had to use the bathroom. She slid her phone into the pocket of her dress—one of the best innovations in recent years—and stalked toward the double doors leading to the hallway. She nodded at Kayla as the fairy lights in the school gym made her dress dazzle beautifully. Kayla nodded back, stepping away from their table and engaging Mr. Pombom, one of the ball's chaperones, in a conversation to distract him.

Violet pushed open the double doors and softly pulled them closed. She didn't want to make any unnecessary noise or draw attention to herself. Luckily, she had perfected the art of being invisible. One perk of being the good girl… the quiet girl. Her heart seemed to thump loudly in her chest and she could have sworn it echoed throughout the empty halls. Of course, she knew it was only her wild imagination.

Violet headed to the computer lab, which she unlocked using the key Savannah had swiped from the janitor the day before. Before entering the computer lab, she glanced down the hall and quietly shut the door. She flicked on the light switch. As light flooded the room, she sat in front of a computer and powered it on. Sometimes having a brother who was a computer nerd and spent most of his day online came in handy.

Violet completed the next phase of the plan, left the computer lab, and locked the door behind her. Now she only hoped Kayla could distract Mr. Pombom long enough for them to get away with it.

Several minutes later, Violet re-entered the gym and returned to the table she had claimed earlier. Jess wasn't there anymore, but she would worry about that in a minute. She texted Savannah and Kayla in the group chat.

**Violet:** It's done.

**Savannah:** Starting the next phase!

Kayla didn't reply, but Violet looked around the room and noticed she was still talking to Mr. Pombom. Good.

Violet fidgeted with the tulle on her dress, glancing around the gym for Jess. She spotted him talking to some guys on the basketball team. That was fine, as long as he was in the room.

Right on time, the projector screen began to descend from the ceiling. Violet knew Savannah had pushed the button to reveal it for the next part of their plan. The screen flickered to life and Mallory appeared on-screen, her icy blue eyes glinting with anger. She was sitting in her bedroom, her legs curled beneath her as she sat propped against an elegant mahogany headboard.

"I don't care if my dad is having an affair with Izzy's mom." She rolled her eyes. "He paid me $5,000 not to tell anyone. I know you won't do anything about it, so you don't count. It's not like it matters. My parent's marriage is falling apart. He might as well enjoy himself if my mom won't give him what he needs."

A female's voice with a strong southern accent responded from behind the camera. Savannah. "You might not care about your parents, but what about Izzy's dad? Doesn't he deserve to know the truth? Are you so sure that your mom doesn't deserve that too?"

Mallory laughed darkly and swept her black hair behind her ears. "What's the point? No one deserves the truth. It's better this way, trust me. They would all rather be in the dark about it and act like their lives are perfect, rather than the fucking messes they are."

The screen went black for a few seconds, then another video clip started playing. This time, it showed Mallory and Rose standing beside a row of lockers, with Violet standing across from them.

"You're such a dumbass you can't even stand up for yourself. How pathetic. No wonder no one likes you. The world would be better off without you. You should probably just run off and *kill yourself*," Mallory said, spitting out each word viciously as she stepped closer to Violet.

Rose gasped, but she quickly tried to compose herself and hide her shock at Mallory's words.

"You bitch." Tears sprang to Violet's eyes as she finally snapped.

Violet struck Mallory across the cheek. Despite the noise of the raucous students around them, the sound of the slap echoed through the speakers.

The screen went black for a few seconds again, then showed a third video clip. By this point, most people had gathered around the projector to watch. People were whispering and gossip was starting about who had set it up. Violet heard her own name whispered and saw glances her way as people hypothesized who would do such a thing.

The third clip showed Kayla in her emerald green dress walking over to a bed, then sitting down. Violet prepared herself, knowing this one would be difficult to watch for multiple reasons. Jess was in the room with Kayla. It was the night of Mallory's sixteenth birthday party.

The clip played out, with Jess admitting he poisoned Mallory's drink while grinning manically. Suddenly, Kayla pulled out her knife, but Jess lunged forward, wrestled the knife from Kayla, and stabbed her in the stomach. In the tussle, his black mask covered in silver swirls fell to the floor. Several minutes later, Jess left the room and Kayla crawled to grab her phone, then the screen went black yet again.

Kayla had told Violet she set her phone to record when she went into the bedroom with Jess because she was scared of what he would try, and she wanted evidence in case something happened. She had been terrified about exposing the truth, but she and Violet both knew the truth was worth telling and that Jess needed to be taken down for what he had done.

Violet spotted Mallory slowly, painfully, crossing the room with her crutches. She wore a mermaid-style lime green dress that showed off her midriff. An intense expression of horror splayed across Mallory's normally pretty face. She was most likely livid about her secrets being revealed in front of most of the school. Izzy, Savannah, and Rose accompanied her, while her brother Jack was close behind. Despite her extensive injuries, Mallory apparently hadn't wanted to miss the fall ball. Savannah had told Violet and Kayla beforehand, so they were aware. Mallory couldn't bear the thought of missing out on an important school event. She assumed she would be the center of attention, and Savannah had told them she would be vying for everyone's sympathy. It was too perfect.

But this wasn't the end.

# Chapter 39:
# After Jess

*November 16, 2019*

The projector screen rolled back up. Mr. Pombom had rushed away in the middle of the "presentation," so, presumably, he was the one who turned off the projector. It wasn't the end of the evidence they had compiled, but hopefully it was enough to condemn Jess and Mallory. Violet hoped Savannah had left the projector room before she was caught.

Someone tapped on her shoulder and she whipped around uneasily, but it was only Kayla.

Kayla grinned. "That went well."

"As well as we could have expected. Ready for the grand finale?"

Violet's gaze drifted to where Jess had been standing next to some basketball team members earlier, but he was gone. She wondered if he had left while the videos were playing. It didn't matter. They needed to finish this tonight.

Violet pushed a few loose strands of hair behind her ears. "Let's go."

Violet and Kayla left the gym together. This part of their plan required them both. Violet was still nervous about what would happen if someone figured out what they did, but she didn't want to back down. She wanted revenge. Terrible people shouldn't get away with doing terrible things. Where was the fairness in that? The world needed people like her and Kayla to set the world right and enact justice.

Even though homecoming had been recently, the fall ball was another school dance where a queen and king were crowned. Mallory had been the homecoming queen and Stefan, a boy on the football team, had been homecoming king. However, now that Violet and Jess were publicly a couple, no one knew who would be crowned fall ball queen and king. Violet and Kayla hoped it would be Mallory and Jess. They used to date and had supposedly been the hottest power couple in the school. They were both still popular, even if Jess seemed to think he was a social pariah. Most of their peers loved him and would probably vote for him. On the other hand, people would probably vote for Mallory just to avoid her wrath.

The crowning ceremony and announcement were coming up soon, so Violet and Kayla hurried backstage. They were the invisible outcasts, so no one noticed as they entered the backstage area and headed toward the plush red curtains that were currently closed. Kayla was friends with Lukas, the guy in charge of audio for most school events, so they knew they were safe.

Violet listened as Principal Collins rambled on and on about school spirit, how beautiful fall was in Asheville, and how important this dance was—and that it wasn't just a dance, but a symbolic representation of growth, prosperity, and an opportunity for students to stand united as one. Kayla mimed gagging as she made eye contact with Violet and they both laughed.

Kayla stood near the curtains and held a silver lighter in her gloved hand. She had convinced Lukas there wouldn't be any audio issues and sent him away, since the announcements were almost over. He had agreed to leave. He was probably all too eager to leave early, since he had been standing there all night and missed the best parts of the ball.

They waited a few more minutes for the fall ball queen and king to be announced.

"...And this year's fall ball queen and king are Mallory McKenzie and Stefan Rhodes!" Principal Collins spoke much too loudly into the microphone in his excitement, causing a horrific screeching noise to spread throughout the speakers in the room.

Violet gasped as she noticed what had happened, but the flames were already spreading across the curtains. They hadn't considered that the curtains were old and the fabric probably hadn't been replaced or cleaned in years. Decades of dust and debris made the curtains go up in flames almost instantly. Earlier in the night, Savannah had doused the curtains in nail polish remover. Mallory always kept some in her locker so she could fix her nails during the school day, so Savannah had taken it out of her locker before the fall ball started.

Plus, they had used Jess's lighter to start the fire. If the principal, firefighters, or any law enforcement investigating the fire found the nail polish remover and discovered the source of the fire, then they could trace it back to Mallory and Jess.

Violet grabbed Kayla's hand and pulled her toward the exit. They hastily left, not bothering to go back into the gym to watch what would happen. It was better if they got out of there as quickly as possible.

"Shit!" Kayla exclaimed as Violet sat in the passenger seat of her car panicking.

Kayla threw the car into reverse and sped out of the school's parking lot. "Where should we go? Your house?"

Violet bit her lip. "Uh, sure. I can't believe Jess didn't win. How bad do you think the fire will be?"

"I'm not sure, but I'm glad we got out of there fast. Hopefully, no one saw us besides Lukas."

Violet's phone buzzed with a text.

**Savannah:** OMG you guys!! What happened?!

**Violet:** What's going on? We left when we heard that Mallory and Stefan won queen and king.

**Savannah:** You left?! So, you missed it? The curtains completely went up in flames and there was like an explosion that took down Mallory and Collins. Stefan wasn't onstage yet when it happened. I have no idea where Jess was, though.

"What's going on? Who texted you?" Kayla continued driving and glanced uneasily at Violet.

"Savannah said the curtains went up in flames and there was an explosion that took down Mallory and Principal Collins. I'm not sure if she was being overdramatic or not."

"Holy shit! Do you think they're injured or—" Kayla didn't finish the thought.

"Well, if they are, isn't that what we wanted?"

She wasn't sure now. Had they done the right thing? Jess was supposed to be the one onstage, not Stefan. Principal Collins was a necessary but unfortunate casualty. But they hadn't planned on killing anyone, just scaring Mallory and Jess enough that they backed off. Oh God. What had they done?

# Chapter 40:
# After Jess

*Four months later*

It was finally over. Jess and Mallory had gotten what they deserved. Mallory ended up switching to a private school after the incident. Second-degree burns covered her body from the fire, but after her parents hired the best plastic surgeon available, she recovered to her regular, beautiful self. Apparently, she couldn't cope with how everyone treated her after the truth came out, so she left the school.

Principal Collins stepped down as principal and took time off work to recover. His face was permanently disfigured, and he had been the one to take the brunt of the fire. Several people claimed to see Mallory shove him in front of her to protect herself. But those could have been rumors.

The Asheville Police Department discovered that the fire at the fall ball was started with nail polish remover and a lighter. The nail polish remover was proven to have been taken from Mallory's locker. The lighter had Jess's initials carved onto it, and his fingerprints were all over it. Everyone knew about his nasty public breakup with Mallory, so he had a motive to harm her. Most people thought Jess had started the fire, including the police. Violet and Kayla were questioned about the fire because of their friendship with Jess. They stuck to their story that Jess disappeared during the fall ball and they hadn't seen him during the second half of the night, which was true, and implicated him for the crime. Kayla convinced Violet to tell the truth about the stabbing, and she told the police how scared they had been of turning Jess in.

Jess toughed out the situation and continued attending school, almost acting as if nothing had happened. When the police started connecting the dots, they discovered Jess stabbed Kayla and poisoned Mallory. Maybe they would pin him for Jimmy's death, too. Once the police realized Jess and Kayla were friends, and he could have been involved in Jimmy's death, Jess's parents hired one of the top lawyers in NC and were doing everything they could to keep the bad press from affecting their coffee shop. Violet felt sorry for them; they had always been nice to her and seemed like good people, but they hadn't noticed what their son was up to or realized that he was capable of such dark things.

Violet and Kayla were closer than ever. They spent nearly every weekend together, ate lunch together at school, and were almost inseparable, unless Kayla was with Glenn. Kayla and Glenn had officially started dating, which was weird. Still, they seemed happy together, so Violet was happy for them. Kayla managed to pull Glenn out of his room and away from video games. She had even convinced him to get a job working at a local retail store that sold video games and board games.

Violet was single, and she wasn't sure when she would be ready to date again. Jess hadn't taken the breakup well and had harassed her, so her dad had installed a top-of-the-line security alarm and surveillance system outside their house. Violet finally told her dad everything, and she wished she had found the courage to tell him sooner. She had endured enough dating nightmares to last a lifetime. Violet wondered when she would be ready to take a chance on someone new, but until then, she felt content with her social life for the first time in years. She had stood up for herself. It was a good feeling, one she hoped would last.

The best part of all the craziness was that Mallory had transferred schools. Violet no longer felt like she had to constantly watch her back. Of course, she felt guilty about what had happened to Principal Collins, but whenever she brought it up, Kayla reminded her how he had treated Violet when Mallory was bullying her. He had let the bullying continue. And didn't that mean he deserved what had happened to him? Didn't everyone get what they deserved in the end?

When Violet entered Big Beanz for the first time in over four months, she confidently strode over to the counter to place her regular iced coffee order. She hadn't been to the coffee shop since she and Jess were together, but she had tried to convince herself it was necessary to prove she was fully over him. If she saw him, then so be it. She was fine without him. In fact, she was better off. In a weird, messed up way, dating Jess had given her confidence. She had learned what she was capable of.

As she stepped to the side so the next person in line could order, she spotted Jess walking out of the kitchen. When he saw her, he headed toward her.

"Hey," he said softly; his green eyes looked down at her earnestly.

"Hey." She wouldn't let him get to her, despite everything that had happened between them.

"How have you been?"

Violet laughed sarcastically and shook her head. "You can't imagine what I've been through."

"This hasn't been easy on me either, you know. I'm dealing with so much shit from my parents and the—the local police."

"I heard about that."

"Were you at the ball when it started? The fire, I mean?" Jess asked, with a curious expression.

"No, Kayla and I left early," she said carefully.

He stared at her as if he was debating his next words. "It wasn't you, was it?"

"I guess you'll never know."

Jess shook his head and smiled ruefully. He wasn't stupid, but Violet hoped he was smart enough to let it go. He knew what she was capable of. "I really am sorry about—well, about everything. I wish it had ended differently between us."

"You're only saying that now that you're single and lonely. You were never content with what you had. I don't think you were happy when you were with Mallory, either. I'm still not sure why you dated me when you could have dated a dozen other girls at school."

"I cared about you, Violet. I still do."

"Iced coffee for Violet!" the employee working the front counter yelled.

"I better go get my drink." Violet walked toward the pick-up counter, but she turned to look at Jess one last time. "Good luck with the trial. I hope you get what you deserve." She gave an innocent smile.

Jess glared at her, his green eyes darkening as he moved closer to her. "If this trial doesn't end in my favor, then you're going to regret it."

# Acknowledgements

As with every book, I have so many people to thank for helping me along the way. Being an indie author can feel lonely at times, but it's definitely not a solitary process.

First, I'm so thankful for my wonderful, wonderful husband Zed. He's the one who painstakingly formats each of my books. He dealt with me spending countless nights writing, editing, marketing, researching self-publishing, and endlessly talking about book-related things. He also helped me get through the immense stress and anxiety of having 2 fewer weeks for editing, because of an editor who ghosted me. I couldn't do any of this without his unwavering support and love.

Mandi Lynn, who owns Stone Ridge Books, has designed all four of my beautiful book covers. She has helped me bring my visions to life with her creativity and artistic talent.

Melanie, owner of Get It Write Editing Co., saved this book after a very unfortunate incident with another editor. Melanie squeezed my book into her editing schedule and met my extremely quick deadline, which ensured I could publish the book on the planned release date.

My amazing beta readers: Alex, Robert, and Ren. Your valuable feedback helped me shape this book into something even better than I imagined. Thank you for always reading my early drafts and for being honest with me about what needs to be changed.

And last but not least, to you, my readers. The ones who have been there since the beginning. The ones who anxiously waited for my first young adult book. The ones who messaged me, emailed me, or commented on my posts asking when it would be released. The ones who posted a book review, shared my social media posts, told your friends and family about my books, and helped spread the word that my books are worth the read. The ones who just discovered my books. All of you. Thank you.

## Note from the Author

If you want to help me, I would appreciate it immensely if you wrote an honest review for *The Quiet Girl*. Posting your review online is one of the best ways to support indie authors. Reviews help other readers decide which books they want to buy and allow indie authors to gain more exposure to new readers. Please consider posting an honest review on the book retailer website where you purchased the book and/or on Goodreads.